COLTON RESCUE

Marie Ferrarella

HARLEQUIN®ROMANTIC SUSPENSE

Special thanks and acknowledgment are given to Marie Ferrarella for her contribution to The Coltons of Red Ridge miniseries.

ISBN-13: 978-1-335-45622-9

Colton Baby Rescue

Copyright © 2018 by Harlequin Books S.A.

Recycling programs for this product may not exist in your area.

Printed in U.S.A.

www.Harlequin.com

Books by Marie Ferrarella

Visit the Author Profile page at
Harlequin.com for more titles.

To

Nancy Parodi Neubert

And

The Successful Return

Of

Happiness

Chapter 1

He *really* did not have time for this.

Detective Carson Gage frowned as he drove down the darkened streets to The Pour House. He had more important things to do than attend his older brother Bo's bachelor party at a second-rate dive bar in the sketchy part of town.

Hell, he would have rather stayed home and spent the evening talking to his K-9 unit partner, Justice. Granted it would have only been a one-way conversation, but the German shepherd was probably more intelligent than half the people who were going to be at the bachelor party anyway.

This whole thing was a joke, the Red Ridge police detective thought. Bo shouldn't be getting married anyway, not to a woman who he'd only known for a total of three months. This was way too sudden.

The whole thing seemed rather strange to him, not to mention ironic. Bo's bachelor party was being thrown at The Pour House, which just happened to be owned by Rusty Colton, who was the father of Bo's last girlfriend, Demi—the woman Bo had been engaged to for one month, then dumped when he took up with Hayley Patton, his current bride-to-be.

More than likely, Carson thought dourly, given who was being invited to this party, the evening was going to end up in a huge brawl—which was why he intended to stay for just one drink, then get the hell out of there.

Besides, he had work to do. His burning obsession was to find some piece of irrefutable evidence he could use to finally put away the Larson brothers, the cold-blooded twins who fancied themselves up-and-coming crime lords intent on building up a vast criminal empire and destroying everything and everyone in their path.

The Larsons were behind at least two murders that he knew of and they were at the center of a rash of drug busts, but because the thugs who worked for the brothers were more afraid of them than they were of the police, he hadn't been able to find anyone willing to testify against the twins.

But he would. Come hell or high water, he would, Carson swore, his hands tightening on his car's steering wheel. All he needed was to find that one elusive piece of evidence that would start the process of nailing the Larson brothers' coffins shut.

Carson picked his way through the streets, driving slowly. The area seemed even more unsavory at this time of night than it was during the day.

"If you *have* to marry this one, why couldn't you just run off and elope like a normal guy?" Carson asked out loud, addressing the brother who wasn't there. "Why all this need for fanfare and hoopla?"

It almost seemed, what with having the bachelor party at The Pour House, like Bo was deliberately rubbing Demi's nose in his wedding.

Yup, fireworks were definitely going to be on the agenda tonight, Carson thought. One beer and he was out of there, he promised himself again. He had no burning desire to break up a bunch of drunken men who should know better, doing their damnedest to knock each other's heads off. Bo had said he was inviting both Coltons and Gages to this party. Gasoline and fire, Carson thought.

He swore under his breath. No, he definitely didn't need this.

With a sigh, he pulled into The Pour House's parking lot. Because he wanted to be able to drive off the lot with a minimum of maneuvering—*and* make sure that his car didn't get dented by some celebrant who had overindulged in liquid courage, Carson decided to park all the way in the back of the lot. It would be a bit of a trek to the bar's front door, but it was between that and his peace of mind, and his peace of mind definitely made it worth it.

So he guided his vehicle all the way to the last row of the lot. The lot happened to back up against a grassy embankment.

Pulling up the hand brake, he sat there for a while, trying to get into the right frame of mind.

It wasn't happening.

With a sigh, the police detective got out of his car and locked it. Carson was about to start walking toward the entrance of the bar when he thought he saw someone lying facedown at the very far edge of the lot.

Carson paused, squinting. That part of the parking lot was pretty dark. What streetlights there were didn't reach that far.

"Looks like someone's already been partying too much," he muttered under his breath.

Some people just couldn't pace themselves accordingly and this guy obviously couldn't hold his liquor, Carson thought. With a resigned sigh, he changed course and headed toward the drunk instead of the bar. If he didn't wake the guy up and get him out of the way, Carson had no doubt that during the course of the evening, someone was liable to run the drunk over.

The lot wasn't all that full yet, he observed. This guy must have got a *really* early start. From what he could make out, the man was half on the edge of the lot, half on the grass at the very perimeter of the parking lot.

Drawing nearer, Carson saw that the man, whose face was obscured because it was turned toward the grass, had one arm stretched out with his index finger raised, like he was trying to draw attention to something.

That's odd.

And then, despite the fact that it was pretty dark there, Carson saw that there was writing on the ground just above the man's head. It looked as if he had written something—

In blood?

Taking his phone out, he hit the flashlight app, then squatted down. Using the light from his phone, Carson looked at the ground just above the man's head more closely.

"It looks like you wrote *Demi C*," Carson murmured, half to himself. The last letter was barely finished.

Demi C? Demi Colton?

Carson's eyes widened. What was this guy doing, writing the name of his brother's former girlfriend on the parking lot asphalt? And where had the blood come from? Had the guy hit his head?

"Hey, fella, wake up. The parking lot's no place to take a nap." He shook the man's shoulder but couldn't seem to rouse him.

Blowing out a breath, Carson rose to his feet and

circled the man's body so he could get a look at the drunk's face.

"C'mon, fella, you can't sleep it off here. You've gotta get—"

The rest of the sentence froze on Carson's lips.

The man he was trying to wake up was his brother. Bo's eyes were wide-open and unseeing.

There was a black cummerbund stuffed into his mouth. And he wasn't breathing.

Chapter 2

Detective Carson Gage's hands were shaking as he urgently turned his brother over onto his back. Any hope of trying to revive Bo disappeared the moment he saw the bullet wound.

His brother had been shot right through the heart.

Irrationally, Carson felt for a pulse anyway. There was none. Swallowing a curse, he sat back on his heels. His brother's skin was already cold to the touch. This was January in Red Ridge, South Dakota, but death brought a different sort of cold with it and there was no mistaking it for a simple reaction to the weather.

"Damn it, Bo, I *told* you playing fast and loose with women would be the death of you someday. Why d'you have to prove me right?" Carson demanded angrily.

He curbed his impulse to straighten Bo's clothing. Bo always took pride in his appearance and death had left him looking disheveled. But the crime scene investigators were going to need to see everything just the way he had found it.

Shaken to the core, Carson got back up to his feet and opened up his cell phone again. He needed to call this in.

It took him a minute to center his thoughts. He was a trained police detective, Carson silently upbraided himself. He couldn't afford the luxury of coming apart like some hysterical civilian who had just unexpectedly witnessed death up close and personal—even if this *was* his half brother.

Taking a deep breath and then exhaling, he put in a call to his chief, Finn Colton. As he waited for Finn to pick up, he looked again at the name his brother had written in his own blood.

Demi C.

Demi Colton. Carson shook his head. When this got out, it was going to throw all of Red Ridge into one hell of an uproar, he thought. As if the feud between the Coltons and the Gages needed more fuel.

The next moment, he heard Finn's deep voice as the chief answered his phone. "Hey, Gage, aren't you supposed to be at your brother's bachelor party right now, getting drunk and toasting Bo's last few hours of freedom? What are you doing calling me?"

Carson enunciated the words carefully, afraid that if he spoke any faster, his voice was going to break. He and Bo weren't close, but they were still family. "There's been a murder, Chief."

"Damn," Finn cursed. Instantly, the voice on the other end became serious. "Whose?"

Carson paused before answering. "Bo's."

"This your idea of a joke, Gage?" Finn demanded impatiently. "'Cause if it is, it's not funny."

"I only wish it was, Chief," Carson answered.

"You're serious," Finn responded, stunned. When no contradiction came, Finn asked, "Where and when?"

Carson looked down at his brother's body. The whole scene seemed utterly surreal to him. "I just found him two minutes ago, lying facedown at the edge of The Pour House's parking lot."

"The Pour House," Finn repeated. "Isn't that where his bachelor party is supposed to be taking place tonight?"

"One and the same," Carson answered his superior numbly. He realized he was leaving the most important part out. "And, Chief?"

"Yeah?"

"Looks like Bo wrote a name in his own blood. Maybe his killer's name."

Carson heard a noise on the other end as the other

man said something unintelligible before going on to ask, "Whose name did he write?"

"Demi C."

This time there was total silence on the other end for approximately thirty seconds as the information sank in.

The city of thirty-five thousand citizens had more than its share of Coltons. There were three branches in total, as different from one another as the seasons were. The chief liked to say that he belonged to the middle branch, the one that was neither rich nor poor and rough around the edges.

But whatever section he gravitated to, the chief was still a Colton and Carson couldn't help wondering how Finn Colton would deal with having to bring in one of his own as a suspect for first-degree murder.

Finally, the chief broke the silence and asked, "You think Bo wrote that?"

"It's in his own blood, Chief," Carson answered. Then, in case there was any further question as to whether or not Bo was the one who wrote the name, he added, "There's blood underneath Bo's fingernail. Looks like he wrote it."

Finn sighed as if the weight of the world had suddenly been dropped on his shoulders.

"Good enough for me," he replied. "I'll have Demi brought in for questioning. Meanwhile, I'll send some of the team to bring in your brother's body." His voice softened, as if he was feeling sympathetic about what Carson was going through. "You can give your statement in the morning if you need some time, Gage."

Finn was cutting him some slack, Carson thought. He didn't want any slack, he wanted to get his brother's killer.

Now.

"I don't need any time, Chief." Somewhere in the distance, a coyote howled. Carson would have been hard-pressed to name a lonelier sound. "I'll stay here with Bo until the detail gets here," he told his boss. "And then I'm coming down to the station. I want to be there when you interrogate Demi."

"Gage, you can't—"

Carson felt the walls going up. He cut Finn off before the chief could officially exclude him. "I *need* to be there when you question her, Finn. You owe this to me, Chief."

There was silence again. An annoyed silence if he was any judge, Carson thought. He fully expected the chief to argue with him, but he wasn't about to back down.

However, Finn surprised him by saying, "All right, you can be there, but I'll be the one handling the interrogation. I don't want to hear a word out of you, understood?"

Even though Finn couldn't see him, Carson nodded his head grimly. "Understood."

Terminating the call, Carson put his phone into his pocket. Silence enshrouded him although the distant sound of music and raised voices coming from the bar sliced through the air, disrupting the night.

"Sounds like your bachelor party's getting underway without you," Carson said to the prone figure near his feet. "Not exactly the way you expected the night to go, is it?" he asked ironically. He squared his shoulders. No, he and Bo hadn't been close, but Bo was still his brother and he didn't deserve this. "Don't worry, Bo. If Demi did this, she'll pay. I don't know what happened, but I promise she'll pay. I'll see to it."

It was getting colder. Carson pulled his sheepskin jacket tighter around him and turned up the collar. But he remained where he was, a guard at his post. He wasn't about to go anywhere until the unit came to pick up Bo's body.

"I know my rights. I'm a bounty hunter, damn it, and I know my rights better than you do," twenty-seven-year-old Demetria Colton shouted angrily at the two police officers who brought her into the small, windowless room within the Red Ridge police station. "Why am I here?" she wanted to know.

But neither of the two police officers, one young, one old, answered her, other than one of them telling her, "The chief'll be here shortly."

"The 'chief'?" Demi repeated in a mocking tone.

"You mean Cousin *Finn*? Is he still pretending to be in charge?"

The two officers left the small eight-by-ten room without answering her. An angry, guttural noise escaped the redhead's lips. Frustrated, she would have thrown something if she'd had something to throw.

"Why am I here?" she demanded again, more loudly this time. Furious, she began to pound on the locked door. "I know you're out there! I demand to be released. You can't hold me here like this, you hear me?" she cried. "I haven't *done* anything, damn it! You let me out of here! Now!"

When the door suddenly opened just as she was about to start pounding on it again, Demi was caught off guard and stumbled backward. Had the table not been right there behind her to block her fall, she would have unceremoniously landed on the floor.

"You're here," her cousin calmly told her as he and Carson walked into the room, acting as if they were about to have a run-of-the-mill, normal conversation, "to answer some questions."

Demi tossed her head, her red hair flying over her shoulder.

"What kind of questions?" she asked defiantly, her dark brown gaze pinning him down.

"Like where were you tonight?" Finn wanted to know, gesturing toward the lone chair on the opposite side of the table and indicating that she should sit.

"Home," Demi bit off, grudgingly sitting down.

"I was in my home—since 5:00 p.m." she added for good measure.

Finn gave no indication whether or not the answer satisfied him. He waited until Carson sat down next to him, then asked, "Alone?"

"Yes," she bit off, then followed that up with a question of her own. "Why?" she demanded. Squaring her shoulders, she drew herself up and raised her chin, always ready to do battle with the world—and her cousin. "Is that a crime now?"

Hearing Carson's chair scrape along the floor as he started to rise, Finn shot him a warning look before answering Demi's question. "No, but murder is."

"Murder," the redhead repeated, growing more furious by the second. She made the only logical conclusion. "You think I *murdered* someone?" she cried, stunned. "And just who is it I was supposed to have murdered?" When Finn didn't answer her immediately, she pounced on him. "C'mon, you can't just throw something like that out and then leave me hanging in suspense, Finn. Just who was it that you think I murdered?"

Unable to remain silent any longer, his hands fisted at his sides, Carson pinned her with a damning look as he answered her question. "Bo. You murdered Bo and then you stuffed a cummerbund into his mouth."

"Bo," she repeated in noncomprehension. And then, for a moment, Demi turned very pale. Her eyes flicked from Bo's brother to her cousin. "Bo's dead?" she asked hoarsely.

It was half a question, half a statement uttered in total disbelief.

Then, not waiting for an answer, what had become known in the county as Demi's famous temper flared, and she jumped up to her feet, her fists banging down on the tabletop.

"You think I killed Bo?" she demanded incredulously, fury flashing in her eyes. "Sure," she said mockingly. "Makes perfect sense to me. The man's dead so let's blame it on the woman he dumped— EXCEPT I DIDN'T DO IT!" she yelled, her angry gaze sweeping over her cousin and her former fiancé's brother.

"Sit down, Demi," Finn ordered sternly. "And calm down."

Instead of listening to her cousin and taking her seat again, Demi Colton remained standing, a firecracker very close to going off in a flash of fireworks.

"*No*, I will *not* calm down," she cried. "And unless you have some kind of concrete evidence against me—" she said, staring straight at her cousin.

"How about Bo writing your name on the asphalt in his own blood?" Finn said. "Demi C."

Demi paled for a moment. "The killer is framing me?"

Finn raised an eyebrow.

Demi gave him a smug look. "Just as I thought. You *don't* have any sort of actual evidence against me. Okay, I'm out of here," Demi declared.

"You'll leave when I tell you to leave," Finn told her sternly. Rising from his chair on the opposite side of the table, he loomed over her.

"*Do* you have any evidence against me, other than my name written in Bo's blood and the fact that I had the bad judgment to have been engaged to the jerk for a month?" she asked, looking from her cousin to the other man in the room.

Though it obviously killed him, Finn was forced to say, "No, but—"

Triumph filled her eyes. "There is no 'but' here," Demi retorted. "You have *nothing* to hold me on, that means I'm free to go. So I'm going." Her eyes swept over her cousin and Carson. "Gentlemen, it has definitely *not* been a pleasure."

And with that, she swept past them to the interrogation room door like a queen taking leave of a pair of disloyal subjects.

Finn shook his head as his cousin stormed out. "Hell of a lot of nerve," he muttered under his breath.

"As I recall, Demi was never the sweet, retiring type. If she was, she would have never become a bounty hunter," Carson told him.

Finn blew out a breath. "You have a point." He walked out of the interrogation room with Carson directly behind him. "Well, check out her alibi, talk to anyone who might have seen her," the chief said, addressing the victim's brother. "I'm open to any further suggestions."

Carson looked at his boss in mild surprise. "I thought you made it clear that I wasn't allowed to work on my brother's case." Although, he thought, since Finn could work on the case in which his cousin was a suspect, he should be allowed to investigate his brother's murder.

"Technically, you're not," Finn said as they walked out into the main squad room. "But I'm not an idiot, Gage. You're going to work this whether I give you my blessing or not." He stopped just before his office. "So you have any ideas where to start?"

He'd been thinking about this ever since he'd found Bo's body. The fact that Bo had written Demi's name seemed pretty damning to him, but he didn't want to discount the slim possibility that someone else had killed his brother.

It didn't warm his heart to have to admit this, but in all fairness, he had to. "Well, it's common knowledge that Demi wasn't the only woman Bo romanced and then dumped. I'd say that there were a whole lot of women who'd love to have seen Bo get what was coming to him. And that includes a number of disgruntled husbands and boyfriends, as well. Why don't we start talking to them?"

That Bo was a playboy wasn't exactly news to

anyone. Finn frowned. "But would any of them actually resort to murder?"

Carson shrugged. Nothing jumped out at him, but this needed closer examination. "Only one way to find out," he told his boss.

"I agree," Finn responded. "Make up a list. Meanwhile, I'm going to have some of the boys go over the crime scene with a fine-tooth comb, see if someone missed anything just in case. Although the ground's undoubtedly been trampled on," he commented.

Carson nodded grimly. "Nobody ever said that solving crimes was easy. I can swing by my place, pick up Justice," he said, referring to his K-9 partner. "See if maybe he can pick up a scent."

"*After* you put that list together," Finn told the detective.

Carson headed over to his desk. Given the hour, the squad room was practically empty. "Will do," he told the chief.

"Oh, and, Gage?" Finn called after him.

Carson turned around, expecting further orders. "Yeah, Chief?"

"I'm really sorry for your loss."

The words were standard-issue, said over and over again in so many instances that they sounded numbingly routine, yet he felt that Finn really meant them.

"Yeah, me, too," Carson answered stoically, then added, "Thanks."

* * *

Carson had just finished making a preliminary list of all the women he could remember Bo having had any romantic encounters with over the last several years when J.D. Edwards, one of the crime scene investigators, came into the squad room. J.D. looked excited.

Temporarily forgetting about the list he'd just compiled, Carson crossed over to the man. J.D., in turn, had just cornered Finn.

"You're going to want to hear this," the investigator was saying to Finn.

The chief, seeing Carson, nodded at him, indicating that he join them. Carson was all ears.

"What have you got?" Finn asked.

"Lots," J.D. answered. "First off, I found this under a wheel near where the body was found." He held up a sealed plastic evidence bag. The bag contained a necklace with a gold heart charm.

Finn squinted as he looked at the necklace. "That looks familiar."

"It should be," the investigator said. "It belongs to—"

"Demi," Carson said, recognizing the gold heart. "That's her necklace."

"And that's not all," J.D. informed them. The investigator paused for effect before announcing, "We've got a witness who says he saw Demi Colton running in the shadows around 6:45 p.m. near The Pour House."

"Six forty-five," Carson repeated. He looked at Finn. "I found Bo's body at seven."

J.D. looked rather smug as he said, "Exactly."

"Who's the witness?" Finn wanted to know.

"Paulie Gains," J.D. answered.

Carson frowned. He would have preferred having someone a little more reliable. "Gains is a small-time drug dealer."

"Doesn't mean he couldn't have seen her," Finn pointed out. He looked at J.D. "How did he know it was Demi? It's dark at that hour."

J.D. laughed. "Not that many people around here have her color hair, Chief."

Finn nodded. J.D. was right. "Okay, that puts her at the scene. Looks like we've got that evidence Demi kept going on about," he told Carson, adding, "Time for that bounty hunter to do some heavy-duty explaining if she intends to walk out of here a second time. Let's go wrestle up an arrest warrant."

Carson didn't have to be told twice. He led the way out the door.

Chapter 3

It took a little time, but Carson and his boss finally found a judge who was willing to issue an arrest warrant at that time of night.

"Do me a favor, lose my number," Judge David Winkler told Finn, closing his front door and going back to his poker game.

Tucking the warrant into his pocket, the chief turned toward Carson. "Let's go. We're not waiting until morning," Finn told the detective as he got back into his vehicle.

Armed with the warrant, for the second time in less than five hours police detectives hurried back to Demi Colton's small ranch house on the outskirts of town, this time to arrest her.

The house was dark when they arrived.

"I've got a bad feeling about this," Carson murmured as he and Finn approached.

Carson knocked on the door. When there was no response, he knocked again, harder this time. Rather than knock a third time, he tried the doorknob. He was surprised to find that the door was unlocked.

Guns drawn, they entered and conducted a quick room-to-room search of the one-story dwelling. There was no one home.

"Damn it." Finn fumed. "My gut told me to keep her in a holding cell and not let her just walk out of the police station like that."

"Looks like some of her clothes are gone," Carson called out to the chief, looking at a cluster of empty hangers in the bounty hunter's bedroom closet.

"Yeah, well, so is she," Finn answered from the kitchen. When Carson joined him, Finn held up the note he'd found on the kitchen table.

"What's that, a confession?" Carson asked, coming around to look at the piece of notepaper.

"Just the opposite," Finn told him in disgust. "It says 'I'm innocent.'"

Carson said what he assumed they were both thinking. "Innocent people don't run."

The chief surprised him when Finn said, "They might if they think the deck is stacked against them."

"Is that what you think? That she's innocent?" Carson questioned, frowning. He supposed that there was a small outside chance that the chief might be right, but as far as he was concerned, he was going to need a lot of convincing.

"I think I want to talk to her again and find out just how her necklace wound up under the wheel of that car," Finn answered.

In order to talk to the woman again they were going to have to find her. Carson blew out a long breath, thinking.

"Maybe her father knows where she is," he said, speculating. "Won't hurt to talk to him. Man might be able to tell us something."

Although, from what Bo had told him about Demi's contentious relationship with her father, Carson highly doubted that Rusty Colton would be able to give them any viable insight into his daughter's whereabouts.

But, Carson speculated, the old man might know something he didn't know he knew. They had nothing to lose by questioning Rusty Colton.

At least they would be no worse off than they were now, Carson reasoned as they drove over to The Pour House.

The bar's door was closed when they got there, but the lights were still on. Carson banged on it with his fist until Rusty Colton came to unlock it. The tall, skinny man had his ever-present mug of beer in his hand as he opened the door.

Bleary brown eyes quickly assessed the situation from beneath unruly reddish-brown hair.

"Sorry, boys, I'm just about to close up for the night," Rusty said just before Carson pushed his way in. Taking a step back, the bar owner regrouped. "Okay then, I'll have to limit you to just one round— although I just might see my way clear to staying open a little longer if you two boys are willing to pay extra."

Small, beady eyes shifted from the chief to the detective. Rusty waited in anticipation to have his palm greased.

He waited in vain.

"We're not here to drink, Mr. Colton," Carson told the man coldly.

He'd never cared for the owner of The Pour House. There was something palatably unsavory about Rusty Colton. Carson had no doubt that the man would sell his own mother if he needed the money.

Annoyed, Rusty gestured toward the door. "Well then, 'gentlemen,' I need to get back to closing up my establishment," he told them.

Neither of the men moved toward the door.

"We were wondering if you could tell us where your daughter is, Rusty," Finn asked in a voice that said he wasn't about to be trifled with. "Demi."

Rusty snorted. "She's a grown woman, Finn. She comes and goes as she pleases. Ungrateful whelp never did mind me," he said, banging down his empty mug on the counter. "I can't be expected to keep track of her."

Carson moved in a little closer to the man. He wasn't that much taller than Rusty, but he was a great deal more muscular and therefore more intimidating. "You keep track of everything when it suits you. Now, let's try this again," he said evenly. "Where's Demi?"

"Well, if you must know," Rusty said, smugly drawing out each word, "she's gone. Long gone. I think you two apes probably scared her and she high-tailed it out of here."

That wasn't good enough for him. "What makes you so sure?" Carson wanted to know. "Did she tell you?"

"Didn't have to," Rusty answered, pushing together several glasses on the counter in a half-hearted attempt to clean up. "I stopped by her place during my evening break—I leave Amos in charge then. He's dumb, but nobody's going to try to skip out on paying that big ox," he informed the two men at the bar proudly.

"Get back to the point," Finn ordered. "You stopped by Demi's place and then what?"

"Well, she wasn't home so I decided to dip into that big wad of cash she keeps under her mattress like I do every now and then—only when I need a little something to get me through to the end of the month," Rusty admitted without a drop of embarrassment.

"Except that I couldn't this time," he complained. "It was gone. Guess the little witch must have taken it and hightailed it out of here." He looked quite put out by his youngest daughter's action. "Didn't even think to leave me any, my own daughter," he complained.

Carson exchanged looks with his boss. They weren't going to get anything more out of Rusty.

"Let us know if she comes back," Finn told the man as he walked out.

Rusty grunted something in response, but it was unintelligible and they'd already lost too much time, Carson reasoned, following the chief out.

"Warrant's not going to do us any good right now," Carson bit out, handing the paper back to Finn.

"I'll put out an APB on her," Finn said, striding back to his vehicle. "Maybe we'll get lucky. In the meantime, have the team look into those people whose names you wrote down."

Frustrated, Carson nodded as he got into the car. For now, at least it was a place to start.

Early the following morning, Carson stood by as the chief called a staff meeting of all the K-9 cops and gave them instructions. Articles of Demi's clothing, got from her house, were handed out in order to give the dogs a scent to track.

Others on the force got busy looking into Bo's

past. The latter included interviewing women Bo had seen, exploring the various gambling debts he ran up and, since Bo had been an in-demand dog breeder who'd trained and sold dogs to people and organizations besides the police department, Carson started conducting a second background check on those people. Maybe there was a disgruntled client out for revenge and the situation had got out of hand for some reason.

It was time-consuming and grueling and it all ultimately led nowhere.

Serena Colton absolutely refused to buy into all the lurid hype surrounding her cousin Demi.

Here, tucked away in her private wing of her parents' vast, prosperous Double C Ranch, the story of Bo Gage's murder and how *Demi C* was found written in Gage's own blood beside his body sounded like the fanciful imaginings of a second-rate scriptwriter. Except that Bo Gage *was* found murdered and Demi's name *did* appear to be written next to his body.

"I don't believe it," Serena said to her three-month-old daughter, who was dozing in her arms. "There's *got* to be another explanation for this, Lora. Sure, Demi has her shortcomings," she readily admitted, "but she's not a murderer."

Serena sighed, gently rocking her daughter as she restlessly paced around the very large bedroom. "You take all the time in the world growing up, Lora, you hear me? Stay little for as long as you can. And I'll do my part. I won't let anything like this ever touch you," she whispered to the sleeping child. "I'll keep you safe, little one. I promise."

As if to challenge the promise she had just made to her daughter, the sound of approaching sirens pierced the night air.

The sirens grew progressively louder, coming closer.

Worried, Serena moved to the window facing the front of the house and looked out. She was just in time to see the headlights from two police vehicles approaching the house—mansion, really—where she lived with her parents and younger sister, Valeria.

"What could the police possibly want here, and at this hour?" Serena murmured under her breath. Her brother Finn was the police chief and he wouldn't be coming here like this unless there was something very, very wrong—would he? She couldn't help wondering.

As if in response, Lora stirred in her arms. But mercifully, the baby went on sleeping. Although how she didn't wake up with all this noise was a complete mystery to Serena. The sirens had gone silent, but in their wake came the loud, urgent pounding of a fist against the front door.

Her heart was instantly in her throat. The next second, she heard her parents and Valeria all rushing down the stairs to answer the door.

Still holding her daughter in her arms, Serena left her room and went to the landing, hoping to find what was going on from the shelter of the second floor.

She was just in time to see her father throw open the front door. Not surprisingly, Judson Colton looked furious. The tall, strapping ranch owner wasn't accustomed to being treated in this sort of manner.

"Just what is the meaning of all this noise?" Judson Colton demanded even before he had the door opened all the way. When he saw that his own son was responsible for all this uproar, he only became angrier. "Finn! How dare you come pounding on our door in the middle of the night and wake us up like this?" he shouted. "You're not only disturbing me, you're disturbing your stepmother and your sisters as well, not to mention that you're doing the unforgivable and spooking the horses!"

Lightning all but flashed from the man's eyes as he glared at his son and the three men Finn had brought with him. Especially since one of them was holding on to a large German shepherd.

Judson eyed the dog warily. "We raised you better than this, boy," he snapped at Finn indignantly.

"I'm sorry if you're offended," Finn told his father formally. "But this is police business. Murder isn't polite," he added grimly. He and his men had been at this all day. It was nighttime now and he was too tired to treat his father and stepmother with kid gloves.

"Murder?" Joanelle Colton cried, pressing her well-manicured hand against her chest as if trying to hold a heart attack at bay. "This isn't about that man who was found dead outside of that horrid bar, is it?" Finn's stepmother looked from him to Carson. "What does *any* of that awful business have to do with us, Finn?"

"That's what we're here to find out," Finn answered patiently.

Serena had a feeling she knew exactly why they were here.

Carson glanced at the chief. Because this was Finn's family, he needed to absent himself from the immediate search of the house. If there was anything—or anyone—to be found, the chief wouldn't want that to be compromised in a court of law.

"Dan, Jack and I'll search the property," Finn told his father and stepmother. "Detective Gage is going to search the house." He nodded at Carson.

"Search the house?" Joanelle echoed in stunned disbelief. "Search the house for what?" she added indignantly.

But Finn and the two officers he had brought with him had already left the house to start their search.

Taking his cue, Carson, warrant in hand, quickly hurried up the stairs with Justice leading the way.

"Search the house for what?" Judson repeated more forcefully as he followed Carson and his K-9.

"Demi Colton or any sign of her, sir," Carson answered just as he and Justice came to the landing.

He stopped dead when he saw Serena standing there, holding her baby in her arms. At that moment, totally against his will, he was transported to another time and place in his life. He was back in the hospital hallway where a solemn-faced doctor was telling him that he had done everything he could to save her, but Lisa, his girlfriend, had just died giving birth to their daughter. A daughter who wound up dying the following day.

Carson felt an ache form in the pit of his stomach, threatening to consume him even as it undid him.

He struggled to bury the memory again and regain control over himself, just as he had done when his loss had occurred. He'd learned that 99 percent of surviving was just remembering to breathe and put one foot in front of the other.

His voice was gruff and cold as he told the woman standing there, "If you're hiding Demi Colton, now is the time for you to speak up."

On the stairs behind him, Judson cried, "Demi Colton?" He almost laughed out loud at the detective who worked for his son. "You're looking for Demi *here*? Hell, you look all you want, but I can tell you that you're wasting your time. You won't find that woman here."

"If you don't mind, sir," Carson answered stiffly, "I'd like to check for myself."

"Then go ahead and do it, but do it quickly," Finn's father warned. "And see that you don't disturb my daughters any more than you already have. Do I make myself clear, boy?"

"I'd prefer 'Detective,'" Carson replied. Judson Colton merely glared, then turned and went back downstairs.

Finn's stepmother had another sort of complaint to register with him. "Must you bring that mangy creature into my house?" She looked disdainfully at Justice. The canine was straining at his leash.

"Justice is part of the police department, ma'am, same as the rest of us," Carson informed the woman without missing a step.

Rather than cringing or stepping aside, he saw a slight smile grace Serena Colton's lips as she looked down at Justice.

"My father's right, you know. You're wasting your time," Serena told him. "I haven't seen her since yesterday. Demi's not here."

"I need to verify that for myself," Carson told her shortly. "Why don't you go downstairs and wait with the rest of your family?" he suggested.

Carson could feel Judson Colton watching his every move.

"I'd rather stay up here, thank you," Serena answered. "She didn't do it, you know," she told Carson. "Demi's not capable of killing anyone."

Serena was entitled to her opinion, he thought, even though it was naive. "You'd be surprised what people are capable of if they're pushed hard enough," Carson told her.

"There is a limit," Serena insisted.

"If you say so," he replied, complete disinterest in his voice.

His attention was focused on Justice who was moving around Serena's room with growing agitation. Suddenly, Justice became alert and ran up to the walk-in closet. He began pawing at the door.

Carson looked over his shoulder at Serena, disappointment clearly registering on his face. "Not here, huh?"

"No, she's not," Serena insisted, crossing the room to her closet.

Carson waved her back. Taking out his weapon, he pointed it at the closet door and then threw it open. Justice ran in and immediately nosed the hot-pink sweater on the closet floor. The German shepherd moved the sweater over toward his master.

Picking it up, Carson held the sweater aloft and looked accusingly at Serena.

"I said I saw her yesterday," Serena pointed out. "Demi must have dropped her sweater here when I wasn't paying attention. I never said she wasn't here *yesterday*, only that she's not here now—and she isn't," Serena insisted.

Drawn by all the commotion and the headlights from the police vehicles when they drove to the house, Serena's brother Anders, who lived in a cabin on the property and worked as the Double C foreman, came into his sister's bedroom.

"Serena's right. Demi was here at the house yesterday afternoon, but she left and she hasn't been back since. Trust me, I can't abide that little bounty hunter, and I'd tell you if she was here. But she's not," Anders said with finality.

"And neither one of you would know where she went or might consider going if she was running from the police?" Carson pressed.

Serena and her brother answered his question in unison.

"No."

Chapter 4

"Here." Carson shoved the hot-pink sweater over to Anders. "Take this and put it somewhere, will you? The scent is throwing my dog off."

Anders frowned at the sweater Carson had just shoved into his hand. "Sorry. Hot pink's not my color."

Carson wasn't amused by the foreman's dry wit, not when he was trying to find his brother's killer.

"Just get rid of it for now. As long as that's around, Justice can't home in on anything else Demi might have left behind that could wind up proving useful."

Muttering something about not being an errand boy under his breath and looking none too happy about having Carson on the premises, Anders took the sweater and marched out of Serena's suite. Wadding the sweater up, he tossed it into the linen closet that was down the hall and shut the door.

Carson looked back at his dog. Now that the offending piece of clothing was gone, Justice became totally docile.

"C'mon, boy, keep on looking," he urged his German shepherd partner. "Seek!"

Responding to the command, Justice quickly covered the remainder of the upper floor, moving from one area to another, but nothing seemed to spark a reaction from the dog. Nothing caused him to behave as if he had detected any telltale scent that indicated that the woman he was hunting was hiding somewhere on the floor or had even left anything else behind.

Serena kept her distance but still followed the detective, shadowing him step for step. For now, Lora was cooperating and went on dozing.

Coming back through the adjacent nursery, Carson made his way into Serena's oversize bedroom. His eyes met hers.

"See, I told you she wasn't here," Serena told him. When his face remained totally impassive, she heard herself insisting. "You're looking for the wrong person, Detective. Demi didn't kill Bo. There's got to be some kind of mistake."

About to leave her suite and go back downstairs,

Carson stopped abruptly. Justice skidded to a stop next to him.

"My brother's dead. He wrote Demi's name in his own blood on the asphalt right above his head. Her necklace was found at the crime scene, and there's a witness who said he saw Demi running away from the area some fifteen minutes before Bo's body was found in the parking lot. From what I can see, the only mistake here was made by Demi," he informed Serena curtly, doing his best to hold his anger in check.

Part of the anger he was experiencing was because of the crime itself and part of it was due to the fact that having seen Serena holding her baby like that when he'd first entered had stirred up painful memories for him, memories he wanted to leave buried.

Serena shook her head, refusing to buy into the scenario that Demi had killed her ex-boyfriend in some sort of a fit of misguided jealousy. That was not the Demi she had come to know.

"Look," she began, trying to talk some sense into the detective, "I admit that it looks bad right now—"

Carson barely managed to keep a dismissive oath from escaping his lips.

Serena didn't seem to notice as she forged on. "There's no way that the Demi Colton I know is a killer. Yes, she has a temper, but she wouldn't kill anyone, *especially* not her ex-boyfriend."

Carson looked at her sharply. What wasn't she telling him?

"Why?" he questioned.

Did Demi's cousin know something that he didn't know, or was she just being protective of the other woman? Was it simply a matter of solidarity between women, or whatever it was called, or was there something more to Serena's certainty, because she did look pretty certain?

Serena began to say something else, then stopped herself at the last moment, saying only, "Because she just wouldn't, that's all."

Carson looked at the chief's sister closely. She knew something. Something she wasn't telling him, he thought. His gut was telling him that he was right. But he couldn't exactly browbeat her into admitting what she was trying to hide.

He was just going to have to keep an eye on the chief's sister, he decided.

Just then, the baby began to fuss.

"Shh." Serena soothed her daughter. She started rocking the child, doing her best to lull Lora back to sleep.

But Lora wouldn't settle down. The fussing became louder.

Glancing up, Serena was going to excuse herself when she saw the strange look on the detective's face. In her estimation he looked to be in some sort of pain or distress. Sympathy instantly stirred within her. She hated seeing pain of any kind.

She had to be losing her mind, feeling sympathy for a man who seemed so bent on arresting her cousin. It was obvious that he had already convicted Demi without a trial and looked more than willing to drag Demi to jail.

However, despite all this, for some strange reason, she was moved by the underlying distress she saw in his eyes.

"Is something wrong, Detective Gage?" She waited for him to respond, but he didn't seem to hear her despite their close proximity. "Detective Gage?" she said more loudly.

Suddenly realizing that she was talking to him, Carson looked at the chief's sister. She seemed to be waiting for him to respond to something she'd obviously said.

"What?" he all but snapped.

The man was in no danger of winning a congeniality award, Serena thought. "I asked you if something was wrong."

Damn it, Carson upbraided himself, he was going to have to work on his poker face. "You mean other than the obvious?"

Serena mentally threw up her hands. This was hopeless. Why did she even care if something was bothering this boorish man who had come stomping into her house, disrupting everyone without displaying so much as an iota of remorse that he was doing it. Never mind that her brother had led this invasion into her parents' home, she felt better blaming the detective for this than blaming Finn.

"Never mind," she told Carson, changing topics. "I have to see to my baby, if it's all right with you," she said, a mild touch of sarcasm breaking through.

Rather than say anything in response, Carson just waved her back to her quarters.

Serena's voice was fairly dripping with ice as she said, "Thank you."

With that she turned on her bare heel to walk back into her suite.

"Let's go, Justice," Carson said to the dog, steering the animal toward the stairs.

Keeping a tight hold on the dog's leash, Carson walked out of the house quickly, a man doing his best to outrun memories he found far too painful to coexist with.

Once outside, he saw the other members of the K-9 team. Not wanting to be faced with unnecessary questions, he forced himself to relax just a little.

"Anything?" Carson asked the man closest to him, Jim Kline.

Jim, paired with a jet-black German shepherd whimsically named Snow, shook his head. "If that woman's anywhere on the property, she's crawled down into a gopher hole and pulled the hole down after her," the man answered him.

Finn came over to join them. Carson noticed that the chief looked as disappointed as he felt.

"Okay, men, everybody back to the station. We're calling it a night and getting a fresh start in the morning." The chief glanced over in his direction. "You, too, Gage," he ordered, obviously expecting an argument from Carson.

And he got it. "I'm not tired, Chief," Carson protested, ready to keep going.

"Good for you," Finn said sarcastically. "Maybe when you get a chance, you can tell the rest of us what kind of vitamins you're on. But for now, I'm still the chief, and I still call the shots. We're going back to the station, end of discussion," Finn repeated, this time more forcefully. He left absolutely no room for even so much as a sliver of an argument.

Resigned, Carson crossed over to his vehicle and opened the rear door to let Justice in. Shutting the door again, he opened the driver's side and got into the car himself.

He felt all wound up. Talking to Serena Colton while she was wearing that frilly, flimsy nightgown beneath a robe that wouldn't stay closed hadn't exactly helped his state of mind, either.

Carson shut the image out. It only got in the way of his thoughts. And despite being dragged through the wringer physically and emotionally, he sincerely doubted he was going to get any sleep tonight.

Biting off an oath, Carson started up his car and headed toward the police station.

Serena could tell that the rest of her family was still up. From the sound of the raised, angry voices wafting up the stairs, they were going on about this sudden, unexpected turn of events and how furious her father and mother were that Finn hadn't seen his way to leaving them out of this investigation strictly on the strength of the fact that they were his family.

Instead, Finn had actually treated them like he would anyone else, rousing them out of their beds just because he felt it was his duty to go over the entire grounds, looking for a woman her parents felt had no business being on the family ranch in the first place.

Serena let them go on venting, having absolutely no desire to get involved by sticking up for Finn. Her parents were going to carry on like this no matter what she said.

Besides, right now her main duty was to her daughter. The ongoing commotion had eventually agitated Lora, and she wanted to get the baby to fall back to sleep.

The corners of her mouth curved in an ironic smile as she looked down at the infant in her arms. Funny how a little being who hadn't even existed a short three months ago had so quickly become the very center of her universe. The very center of her heart.

Since the very first moment Lora had drawn breath, Serena felt obliged to protect the baby and care for her, doing everything in her power to make the world around Lora as safe and inviting for the infant as was humanly possible.

These last few months, her focus had been strictly and entirely on Lora. She had long since divorced her mind from any and all thoughts that even remotely had anything to do with Lora's conception or the man who had so cavalierly—and unwittingly—fathered her.

It had all been one huge mistake.

She had met Mark, whose last name she never learned, at a horse auction. The atmosphere at the auction had been fast paced and extremely charged thanks to all the large amounts of money that were changing hands.

Representing the Double C Ranch and caught up in the excitement, Serena had broken all her own rules that day—and that night. She had allowed the devastatingly handsome, charming stranger bidding next to her to wine and dine her and somewhere amid the champagne-filled evening, they had wound up going back to her sinfully overpriced hotel room where they had made extremely passionate love. Exhausted from the activity and the alcohol, she had fallen asleep after that.

She had woken up suddenly in the middle of the night. When she did, Serena found herself alone, a broken condom on the floor bearing testimony to her drastically out-of-character misstep. Managing to pull herself together and taking stock of the situation, she discovered that the money in her wallet as well as her credit cards were gone, along with her lover.

Canceling the cards immediately, she still wasn't fast enough to get ahead of the damage. Her one-night stand had cost her several thousand dollars, racked up in the space of what she found out was an hour. The man worked fast.

It was a very bitter pill for her to swallow, but she felt that there was an upside to it. She'd learned a valuable lesson from that one night and swore never to put herself in that sort of stupid situation again. Never to blindly trust *anyone* again.

Moreover, she made herself a promise that she was through with men and that she was going to devote herself strictly to raising horses, something she was good at and understood.

That was what she planned.

Life, however, she discovered, had other plans for her. Her first and only one-night stand had yielded a completely unplanned by-product.

She'd got pregnant.

That had thrown her entire world out of kilter. It took Serena a while to gather her courage together to break the news to her parents. That turned out to be one of the worst experiences of her life. They reacted exactly as she had feared that they would. Her father had railed at her, absolutely furious that she had got herself in this sort of "situation," while her mother, an incredible snob from the day she was born, carried on about the shame she had brought on the family.

Joanelle accused her of being no better than her trashy relatives who hailed from the two lesser branches of the family. The only ones in the family who were there for her and gave her their support were her brothers, Finn and Anders.

She also received support from a very unlikely quarter. Her cousin Demi Colton. She and Demi had never been really friendly, given the branches of the family they came from. But Demi had done her a favor involving one of the ranch hands about a year ago. That had earned her cousin a soft spot in Serena's heart.

And then, when she found herself pregnant, with her parents pushing for her to "eliminate" her "shame," it was Demi, surprisingly enough, who had come out on her side. Demi told her that she should do whatever *she* felt she should as long as that decision ultimately meant that she was being true to herself.

At that point, Serena did some very deep soul-searching. Ultimately, she had decided to have her baby. Seeing that her mind was made up, her brothers gave her their full support. However, it was Demi she found herself turning toward and talking with when times got rough.

She wasn't ordinarily the type who needed constant bolstering and reinforcement, but having Demi to talk to, however sporadically, wound up making a world of difference to her. Serena truly believed that it was what had kept her sane during the low points of this new experience she found herself going through.

Because Demi had been good to her when she didn't need to be, Serena wasn't about to turn her back on her cousin just because a tall, good-looking detective wanted to play judge, jury and executioner when it came to her cousin. Demi had obviously fled the area without ever coming to her, but if she had, if Demi had come to her and asked for money or a place to hide, she would have never hesitated in either case.

She believed that Demi was entitled to a fair shake. Most of all, she believed in Demi.

"I wish you would have come to me," she whispered into the darkness. "I wish you would have let me help you. You shouldn't be alone like this. Not now. Especially with the police department after you."

Serena sighed, feeling helpless and desperately wanting to do something to negate that.

Lora began making a noise, her little lips suddenly moving against her shoulder. She was clearly hunting for something.

Three months "on the job" as a mother had taught Serena exactly what her daughter was after.

"You want to eat, don't you?" she said.

Walking over to the rocking chair that Anders had made for her with his own hands, she sat down. Holding Lora against her with one arm, she shrugged out of the top of her nightclothes and pressed the infant to her breast. Lora began feeding instantly.

"Last time, little one," Serena promised, stroking the infant's silky hair. "I'm starting you on a bottle first thing tomorrow morning. Mama's got to get back to doing her job, sweetheart. Nobody's going to do it for her," she told the little person in her arms.

Rocking slowly, Serena smiled to herself. She was looking forward to tomorrow, to getting back to feeling productive. But for now, she savored this very possibly last intimate moment of bonding with her infant daughter.

Chapter 5

As he'd predicted, Carson didn't get very much sleep that night. His brain was too wired, too consumed with reviewing all the details surrounding his brother's murder. There was more than a little bit of guilt involved, as well. He hadn't wanted to go to Bo's bachelor party to begin with, but he still couldn't shake the feeling that if he had only got to it a little earlier, he might have been there in time to prevent his brother's murder from ever happening.

Carson finally wound up dozing off somewhere between two thirty and three in the morning. At least he assumed he'd dozed off because the next thing he knew, he felt hot air on his face. The sensation blended in with a fragment of a dream he was having, something to do with walking through the desert, trying to make his way home with the hot sun beating down on him. Except that he'd lost his way and didn't know just where home actually was.

Waking up with a start, he found Justice looming right over him. The hot wind turned out to be the dog's hot breath. Justice's face was just inches away from his.

Scrambling up into a sitting position, Carson dragged a hand through the unruly thatch of dark hair that was falling into his eyes.

"What is it, boy?" he asked groggily. "Did you solve the crime and couldn't wait to let me know?" Blinking, he looked at the clock on his nightstand. It was a little past six in the morning. How had that happened? "Or are you hungry, and you're trying to wake me up to get you breakfast?"

In response, the four-footed black-and-tan active member of the K-9 police department nudged him with his nose.

"I guessed it, huh?" Carson asked, swinging his legs off his rumpled double bed.

Except for the fact that he had pulled off his boots last night, he was still dressed in the same clothes he'd had on yesterday. He really hadn't thought he was going to be able to fall asleep at all so in his estimation there had been no point in changing out of them and getting ready for bed.

Carson didn't remember collapsing, facedown,

on his bed. He supposed the nonstop pace of the last two days, ever since he'd come across Bo's body in The Pour House parking lot had finally caught up with him.

He blinked several times to get the sleep out of his eyes and focus as he made his way through the condo into his utilitarian kitchen.

"I know what you're thinking," Carson said to the furry shadow behind him. "This whole place could fit into a corner of Serena Colton's suite."

Now, why had that even come up in his haze-filled mind, he asked himself.

Just then another piece of his fragmented dream came back to him. He realized that he'd been trying to cross that desert in order to get back home to Serena.

Home to Serena?

Where the hell had that come from?

He hardly knew the woman. What was his subconscious trying to tell him? It wasn't as if he was in the habit of dreaming about women. When he came right down to it, he hardly ever dreamed at all.

He came to the conclusion that something had to be bothering him about his less than successful interview with Serena last night. At the moment, he just couldn't put his finger on what.

Forget about it for now, he ordered himself. He had something more immediate demanding his attention— and it weighed a little over eighty pounds.

"Okay, Justice. What'll it be? Filet mignon? Lobster? Dog food?" Carson asked, holding the pantry doors open and peering inside at the items on the shelves. "Dog food, it is," he agreed, mentally answering for the dog beside him.

As he took out a large can, Justice came to attention. The canine was watching closely where the can's contents would wind up.

"Don't worry, I'm not going to poach your breakfast," Carson told the dog. "I'm not that hungry."

To be honest, he wasn't hungry at all. But given his present state, he desperately needed a cup of coffee. His brain felt as if it had been wrapped up in cotton and he needed that jolt that his first cup of coffee in the morning brought in order to launch him into his day.

Emptying the dog food into Justice's oversize dish, Carson stepped out of the dog's way as his K-9 partner immediately began to inhale his food. Carson tossed the empty can into the garbage pail in the cabinet beneath his sink and turned his attention to the coffee maker.

He bit off a few choice words. He'd forgotten to program the coffee maker to have coffee waiting for him this morning. Moving over to the refrigerator, he took out the half-empty can of ground coffee and proceeded to make his usual cup of coffee. The end product, thick and rich, was always something that could have easily doubled for the material that was used to repave asphalt. It was just the way he liked it.

Time seemed to move at an incredibly lethargic pace as Carson waited for the coffee to brew and the coffee maker to give off the three high-pitched beeps, signaling that the job was done.

The timer barely finished sounding off before he poured the incredibly thick, sludge-like liquid into his mug. Holding the mug with two hands like a child who had just learned how to drink out of a cup for the first time, Carson quickly consumed the product of his efforts. He drank nonstop until he had managed to drain the mug of its very last drop.

Putting the mug down, Carson sighed as he sat back in his chair. He could almost feel the coffee working its way through his veins, waking up every single blood vessel it passed through with a start.

The fuzziness was definitely gone.

Getting up to his feet, he looked in Justice's direction. The German shepherd had inhaled every last bit of what he'd put into the dog's dish. Carson credited the dog with having the same frame of mind that he did. Justice had needed something to jump-start his day.

"Okay, give me five minutes to shower and change so we can hit the road and get started," he told his furry partner.

As if concurring with what Carson had just said, Justice barked.

Once.

True to his word, Carson was in and out of the shower in less time than it took to think about it. Going to his closet, he found Justice lying on the bedroom floor, waiting for him.

"Don't start nagging me," he told the dog. "I'm almost ready." When the dog barked at him a couple of times in response, Carson said, "Yeah, yeah, I know. I didn't shave." As if in acknowledgement, he ran his hand over what was now beyond a dark five-o'clock shadow. It could have doubled as the inside of an abyss at midnight. "I'll do it tomorrow. There's nobody I'm trying to impress anyway," he added, pulling on a pair of jeans, followed by his boots.

He paired the jeans with a black pullover then put on his go-to navy sports jacket. As a detective, he was supposed to make an effort to dress in more subdued, businesslike attire. This was his effort, he thought drolly.

Adjusting his weapon in its holster, he said, "Okay, Justice, let's roll."

He stopped by the precinct first to see if any headway had been made in the investigation into his brother's murder. Specifically, if there had been any sightings of Demi Colton overnight.

There hadn't been.

When he walked into the squad room, he found that Finn was in the process of handing out the names of people he wanted interviewed in connection with Bo's murder. Names from the list he had compiled for the chief, Carson thought.

"Just in time," Finn said when he saw Carson coming in. "I was beginning to think that maybe you'd decided to take a couple of days off like I suggested."

The chief knew him better than that, Carson thought. "Not until we catch Demi."

When he saw the chief shifting, as if he was uncomfortable, it made him wonder what was up.

"Yeah, well, on the outside chance that it turns out Demi *didn't* kill Bo, we do need to look into other possibilities. Like whether there might be anyone else out there with a grudge against your brother strong enough to want to kill him."

The way he saw it, even thought he had compiled the list for Finn, shifting attention away from Demi would be a waste of time and manpower.

"Bo didn't write anyone else's name in his own blood," Carson pointed out in a steely voice. "He wrote Demi's."

Finn threw another theory out there. "Maybe there was something else he was trying to tell us other than the name of his killer."

Carson frowned. Finn was stonewalling. Everyone knew that things between the Colton and Gage families weren't exactly warm and toasty. There was a feud between the two families that went back a long ways, and it flared up often.

Was that why Finn seemed so intent on running down so-called "other" leads rather than going after a member of his own extended family? Finn was a good police chief, but his behavior seemed very suspicious to Carson.

"I know what you're thinking," Finn said in response to the look he saw descending over Carson's face. "You think I'm trying to protect Demi. I'm not. I'm the police chief of this county. I don't put family above the law. Hell, you were there. I roused my own family out of bed to conduct a search for Demi.

"But I'm not about to bend over backward and behave like someone's puppet just to prove to everyone that I won't let my sense of family get in the way of my doing my job. However, just because half the force is out for blood, doesn't mean I'm going to put blinders on and pretend there might *not* be anyone else out there who stood to gain something from your brother's death."

"Like what?" Carson wanted to know.

"Well, we won't know unless we look into it, will we?" Finn answered. "Now, aside from all those girlfriends your brother was always accumulating before he got engaged to Hayley, he was married once before, wasn't he?"

Carson nodded. "Yeah, to Darby Gage," he told

the chief, adding, "They've been divorced for over two years."

"Which one of them asked for the divorce?" Finn wanted to know.

He didn't have to try to remember in order to answer. "Darby did."

Finn was all ears. "Why?"

A half, rather mirthless smile curved Carson's mouth. Just because he wanted to find Bo's killer didn't mean that he had approved of his brother's fast-and-loose lifestyle.

"Seems that Darby didn't care for the fact that Bo couldn't stop seeing other women even though they were married." He knew how that had to sound to Finn. "I'm not making any excuses for Bo," Carson told the chief. "He was an alley cat. Always had been. And personally, in the end, I think that Darby was glad to be rid of him."

"Maybe she decided she wanted to be *really* rid of him," Finn countered. "In any case, I want you to go talk to the ex-wife. Find out if she has an alibi for the time your brother was murdered."

He should have seen that coming. "Okay, will do," Carson told him. "You heard the man, Justice," he said to the dog. "Let's go."

Since her divorce from Bo Gage two years ago, Darby Gage had been forced to stitch together a number of part-time jobs just to make ends meet.

Carson found her at the diner where she worked the morning shift as a waitress.

It might have been his imagination, but his ex-sister-in-law seemed to tense up when she saw him coming into the diner.

Putting on a cheerful face, Darby walked up to him with a menu and said, "Take a seat, Detective Gage. We've still got a few empty tables to choose from."

Carson picked a table that was off to one side. Parking Justice there, he sat down.

"What can I get you?" Darby asked.

He could see that the cheerfulness was forced. It probably unnerved her to see him here, he guessed. "Answers," he told his ex-sister-in-law.

Her blue eyes swept over him. In his estimation, she looked nervous. She gave up all pretense of cheerfulness. "Is this about Bo?"

His eyes never left her face. His gut told him that she didn't have anything to do with Bo's murder, but he was here so he might as well do his job.

"Yes."

Darby sighed as she shook her head. "I don't know what I can tell you."

"Let me be the judge of that," Carson told her.

He'd found that saying something like that took the reins away from the person he was interviewing and put them back into his hands.

Carson kept one eye on Justice, watching for any

sort of a telltale reaction on the dog's part. All the German shepherds on the K-9 force were initially bred and then trained by Bo or one of the trainers employed at Red Ridge K-9 Training Center. That was actually where his brother had met Hayley, who was one of the trainers.

Bo had made his living breeding the dogs for the police department as well as for other clients. Darby had been part of that business until the divorce and even now, one of her part-time jobs was cleaning the kennels at the training center.

In Carson's experience, German shepherds were exceedingly sensitive when it came to certain character traits and if Darby had somehow been involved in Bo's murder, maybe the dog would pick up on that.

But Justice's response to his former trainer's ex seemed favorable. So much so that when Darby absently stroked the top of the dog's head, Justice wagged his tail.

Taking that into account, Carson still pushed on. "Where were you around 6:30 p.m. the night Bo was killed?" he asked Darby. Then, realizing the waitress might play dumb about the date, he started to add, "That was on—"

"I know when Bo was killed," Darby said, cutting him off. "I was just leaving the kennels after cleaning up at the training center."

Technically, he already knew that because he had got her schedule by calling the places where she worked. But he wanted to hear what she had to say. "Anyone see you?"

"Other than the dogs?" she asked.

He couldn't tell by Darby's expression if she was being sarcastic or just weary. Given that Bo had put her through the wringer and was the reason why she had to hold down all these various jobs just to keep a roof over her head, for now he let the remark slide.

"Yes, other than the dogs."

She thought for a moment. "I think one of the handlers, Jessop, was still there. He might have seen me. To be honest, I didn't think I'd need an alibi so I didn't make a point of having someone see me leave." And then she suddenly remembered. "There's a time card I punched out. That should be proof enough for you."

He knew that there were ways to manipulate a time card. But since, in his opinion, Darby wasn't the type who could even hurt a fly, he nodded and said, "Yes, it should." Getting up from the table, he dug into his pocket and took out five dollars. He put it down on the table. "Thanks for your time, Darby. I'll get back to you if I have any other questions."

Darby picked up the five dollar bill and held it up for him to take back. "You can't leave a big tip, you didn't buy anything," she pointed out.

Carson made no attempt to take the money from her. "I took up your time," Carson answered.

With that he and Justice left the diner.

Chapter 6

Bo hadn't done right by Darby.

That was the thought that was preying on Carson's mind as he drove away from the diner.

They might have been brothers, but he was aware of all of Bo's shortcomings. His older brother had always been the typical playboy: self-centered and careless with anyone else's feelings. He was making good money with his German shepherd–breeding service and could have seen to it that Darby had got a better settlement in the divorce—at least enough so that she wasn't forced to take on so many part-time, menial jobs in order to keep a roof over her head.

But Bo's lawyer had been a good deal sharper than the lawyer Darby had been able to afford to represent her, so Bo had wound up keeping almost everything. He got the house, the business and most of the bank accounts, while Darby had clearly got the very short end of the stick.

In his opinion, the ultimate humiliation was when Bo had tossed her that crumb by letting her earn extra money cleaning out the kennels at his breeding operation.

If his brother hadn't written *Demi C* on the pavement with his blood, Carson might have looked a little more closely at Darby as a possible suspect in Bo's murder. He certainly couldn't have blamed her for being bitter about the treatment she'd received at Bo's hands both before and after the divorce.

But Darby hadn't seemed bitter to him, just closed off. And decidedly weary.

She probably wasn't getting enough sleep, given the various conflicting schedules of the jobs she held down, Carson thought.

"What do you think, Justice?" Carson asked the dog riding in the passenger seat beside him. "You think Darby might have got fed up and decided to teach Bo a lesson for treating her so shabbily?"

Justice barked in response to hearing his name and Carson laughed.

"That's what I thought. You like her, don't you, boy? Back to Demi, then," Carson agreed.

About to drive back to the station, Carson abruptly changed his mind as well as his direction.

He was heading back to the Double C Ranch.

Something had been bothering him about Serena Colton's testimony. *Why* was she so convinced that Demi hadn't killed his brother despite what could be considered a deathbed testimony? Why was she so certain that her cousin wasn't capable of killing someone even though everyone knew the bounty hunter had a bad temper.

He'd once seen Demi take down a man at The Pour House who was twice her size and obviously stronger than she was. Thin and wiry, the woman was nonetheless a virtual powerhouse. Ever since that day, he'd regarded Demi as being rather lethal.

Given that and her unpredictable temper, he'd never thought it was a good idea for his brother to have taken up with her. Demi Colton wasn't the type of woman to put up with being treated the way Bo obviously treated women he was no longer interested in seeing exclusively.

Carson couldn't shake the feeling that there was something that Serena had held back last night when he'd questioned her.

He had no idea if that "something" was significant or inconsequential, but he knew it was going to keep eating away at him until he found out exactly what it was that Serena wasn't telling him. He might as well get this out of the way before he followed up on some of Bo's business dealings and talked to the women he'd romanced and discarded.

* * *

When he arrived at the Double C mansion, Carson debated leaving Justice in his car when he went in. After all, it was January and if he left the windows partially opened, the dog would be all right. However, he regarded Justice as his partner and under normal circumstances, he wouldn't have left his partner just sitting in the car, twiddling his thumbs while he went in to reinterview someone connected to a case.

"You're on your best behavior, boy," he instructed, taking the leash as Justice jumped down out of the passenger seat.

Alma, the housekeeper who opened the front door when he rang the bell, looked far from happy to see him. The older woman cast a wary eye in Justice's direction.

"I'm sorry, Detective. Mr. and Mrs. Colton are not in," she informed him formally.

"That's all right," Carson replied politely. "I'm not here to see them. I'm here to talk to Ms. Colton."

The housekeeper raised her chin as she asked defensively, "Which Ms. Colton?"

The woman knew damn well which one, he thought. She just wanted to make things difficult for him. She was being protective of the people she worked for.

"The older one. Serena," he specified.

The housekeeper frowned. "I'm afraid that she's not here, either."

Just as the woman was about to forcibly close the door on him, Serena's voice was heard calling to her from upstairs. "Alma, I'm going to need you to watch Lora for me for a few hours while I'm working with the horses."

Carson's eyes met the housekeeper's. "Looks like she came back. Lucky me," he commented.

"Yes," the older woman responded icily. "Quite lucky. I will go upstairs and tell Miss Serena that you want to see her."

"That's all right," Carson said, moving past the housekeeper and entering the foyer. "Don't trouble yourself. I can go tell her myself. I know my way."

And with that, he and Justice headed toward the winding staircase.

Carson took the stairs two at a time with Justice keeping pace right behind him.

About to go back into her suite as she waited for the housekeeper to come upstairs, Serena was more than a little surprised to see the detective make his way up to the landing in the housekeeper's place.

Now what? Serena thought impatiently.

"Did you forget something, Detective?" she asked, doing her best to sound polite and not as irritated as she felt.

"No," he answered, reaching the landing, "but you did." He signaled for Justice to sit and the K-9 did.

Her brow furrowed a little as she tried to make sense of what he'd just said. "Excuse me?"

"When we talked last night, I got the feeling that there was something you were holding back, something you weren't saying," he told her. "The more I thought about it, the more certain I was that I was right. I figured I needed to get back to you to find out just what that was." He looked at her expectantly.

Alma had just managed to make her way upstairs. The woman was struggling not to pant. "I'm sorry, Miss Serena. He refused to leave."

"Apparently he's very stubborn," Serena said, looking coldly at the invading detective. She drew herself up, moving away from the bedroom doorway. "Alma, if you don't mind looking after Lora, I'll see if I can't put the detective's mind at rest once and for all, so he can be on his way and we can all go on with our lives."

He waited until the housekeeper picked up the baby from her crib and left with Lora before saying anything to Serena.

"Have I done something to offend you, Ms. Colton?" he asked, referring to her rather abrupt tone.

He had gall, she'd give him that. "You want that alphabetically, chronologically or in order of magnitude?" she asked the detective.

"Tell you what, I'll let you pick," Carson said magnanimously.

He didn't think she was going to say anything, did he, she thought. Well, he was in for a surprise.

Serena launched into him. "You come storm trooping into my house at an ungodly hour—"

"You were up," Carson reminded her.

"That's beside the point," Serena retorted. "I was feeding Lora. But that still didn't give you the right to burst in here—"

"The chief knocked," Carson corrected her. He could see she was getting really frustrated. The fire in her eyes was really rather compelling to watch. "And he is your brother as well as the police chief."

Exasperated, Serena switched to another tactic. "You not only accused a relative of mine of an awful crime but already convicted her in your mind, refusing to even entertain the very real possibility that she wasn't the one responsible for killing your brother."

"I might have 'convicted' her a little too readily," he allowed, "but you absolved her just as quickly despite evidence to the contrary."

"That wasn't actual evidence, it was circumstantial evidence," she insisted.

She was beginning to get to him, not to mention that she was obscuring the real reason why he had returned to the Double C Ranch. "I didn't come here to argue with you."

Serena gave him a knowing look. "You could have fooled me," she retorted.

"I'm not here to do that either," he informed her

curtly, just in case she was going to go off on that tangent. "All I want to know is what you're holding back, Ms. Colton."

She could feel herself losing her temper. "I'm not holding anything back," she protested a little too vehemently.

Carson had no intention of dropping this until he had his answer. "Last night, when you told me that you hadn't seen Demi since the day before—"

"I hadn't," Serena reaffirmed in case he was going to go in that direction.

Ignoring her, he pushed on to get to his point. "You were convinced that cousin of yours wasn't capable of murder."

"She's not," Serena insisted. She was prepared to say that as many times as it took to convince the detective—because she believed with all her heart that it was true.

He wished she'd stop interrupting and let him get to the heart of his case. He glared at her and continued talking.

"When I asked you why you were so certain that she hadn't killed Bo Gage, you looked as if you were going to say something, but then you didn't. You just repeated what you'd already said. What is it that you actually *wanted* to say?"

"You're imagining things," Serena told him dismissively.

Carson's eyes met hers. Immovable, he held his ground.

"No, I'm not," he told her. "Now, one more time. What is it that you were going to say?" He saw the stubborn look that came over her face. She was digging in, he thought. He tried another tactic. "Convince me, Ms. Colton. *Why* couldn't Demi kill my brother?"

Serena shook her head. "I don't—"

"Why?" Carson repeated, more forcefully this time. He gave no sign of relenting or backing off until she gave him an answer.

Serena glared at him, but inside, she was beginning to relent.

It wasn't as if, if she remained silent, all of this would eventually just go away. It wouldn't. There was a very viable piece of evidence of Bo's connection with Demi that wasn't about to be erased. It was only going to grow more prominent with time.

She of all people knew that.

Taking a breath, Serena finally gave Carson what he was after, albeit reluctantly. "Because she wouldn't kill the father of her baby."

"Baby?" Carson repeated, completely stunned. He was definitely *not* expecting something like this. Maybe he'd misunderstood. *"What* baby?"

Was he really being this dense, or did he just want her to spell it out for him, Serena wondered, feeling her anger mounting.

"Demi's baby."

He thought of the woman he had seen not that long ago. Demi Colton had no children. Carson shook his head. "Demi doesn't have a baby."

"Not yet," Serena agreed, feeling as if she had just betrayed the other woman, "but she's pregnant."

He continued to stare at Serena. When he saw her, Demi had been as thin as one of those swizzle sticks they used in bars a class above The Pour House. Was the chief's sister jerking him around, trying to win sympathy for her cousin?

Or was she telling him the truth?

"Demi's pregnant?" he finally repeated.

Serena nodded grimly. "Yes."

He felt like someone trying to find his way through a foggy swamp. "And it's Bo's baby?"

"Yes!" she cried, feeling like a game show host who'd painstakingly led a contestant to the right answer after a number of wrong turns.

Although Bo had been a womanizer, he had never actually bragged about his conquests or talked about them in any sort of detailed manner. To his recollection, Bo had never said anything about getting Demi—or any other woman—pregnant. He would have definitely remembered something like that.

"Did my brother know she was pregnant?" he asked Serena.

"She didn't want to tell him." She saw the quizzical look on Carson's face. "Your brother was going to be marrying another woman. Demi wasn't about to say anything about the baby until after she actually gave birth. She felt that saying something now, right before his wedding, when she wasn't even showing yet would make her look desperate and pathetic in his eyes. Like she was just trying to keep him for herself. Demi had way too much pride for that."

All this sounded somewhat far-fetched to him. "You're sure about this?"

Serena didn't hesitate with her answer. "Very."

She was obviously missing what was right in front of her, Carson thought. "Seems to me that your friend had a very good reason to kill my brother. It's called revenge and it's right up there as one of the top two reasons people kill people," he told her.

Didn't he get it? "You're talking in general, I'm being specific." Serena tried again. "Demi wouldn't kill the father of her baby no matter how much she couldn't stand Bo."

Carson moved his head from side to side as if he was trying to clear it. "You realize that you just proved my point with those last few words you said, right?"

"No," she cried. "I proved mine. Demi wouldn't want her baby to someday hate her for killing its father. She wanted her baby to eventually come to know Bo—and make up its own mind about what a lowlife your brother was," she concluded with feeling.

Carson laughed shortly again as he shook his

head. "You know," he told her, "that almost makes sense—in a weird sort of way."

"The point is," Serena said, "even though she had a temper, Demi was practical. She wouldn't have killed him—she would have waited until the baby was born and then she would have confronted Bo and made sure that your brother lived up to his responsibilities toward the child." She paused, pressing her lips together. It took effort to keep the bitterness out of her voice. "Men can't just have their fun, sowing their seed and disappearing. Not when there's another life involved."

He thought of the baby he saw her with last night. He was aware of Serena's circumstances. "Is that what you told her?"

But Serena shook her head. She wouldn't presume to give Demi advice. "Nobody tells Demi anything. She marches to her own drummer." Serena paused for a moment, her eyes meeting his. "This is just between the two of us."

He thought of Demi. "Seems like there's more people involved than that."

She blew out an exasperated breath. He knew what she meant. "Demi told me this in confidence the last time I saw her. I don't want this getting out, do you understand? I only told you because I wanted you to understand why Demi wouldn't have killed your brother."

He was far from convinced. "If she didn't kill

him, why was his last act before dying to write her name in his own blood?"

"I don't know," she exclaimed. "You're the detective. *You* figure it out. But she didn't kill him," Serena insisted again. "I'd bet my share of the ranch on that."

She looked intense as she said that, and he had to admit that it did rather impress him. "You're that certain?" he questioned.

"I'm that certain," Serena confirmed.

He lifted one shoulder in a half shrug. "I'll keep that in mind. And I'll be getting back to you," he told her just before he walked away.

She didn't win, Serena thought. She hadn't convinced the detective that Demi had nothing to do with Bo's murder. But she could see that she'd created doubt in Carson's mind, which meant that she didn't lose, either. And for now, that was good enough.

Chapter 7

Out for a ride to clear her head a few days later, Serena abruptly reined her horse in.

She stared at the horizon, trying to make out the two riders in the distance, also on horseback.

Ever since Bo Gage's murder, everyone in the area was spooked and on high alert, taking note of anything remotely unusual or out of the ordinary.

Anyone who had business with her father or mother came up the main road to the house, driving a vehicle, not on the back of a horse.

Because she no longer felt as safe these days as she used to, Serena had taken to bringing her rifle with her when she went out for a ride on the range.

She felt that it was better to be safe than sorry and she was quite proficient with a gun.

Her hand went to her rifle's hilt now as she watched the two riders. There was something uncomfortably familiar about them even though she couldn't make out their faces at this distance.

And then she saw Anders coming from the opposite direction. Her brother was riding toward the two men. Even so far away, Serena could tell from his body language that the Double C foreman wasn't happy.

Rather than hang back, she kicked her mare's flanks, urging Nighthawk to head over in Anders's direction. She didn't know why, but something in her gut told her that her brother might need a little support.

And then, as she came closer, she realized why. The two riders she had observed, who were now engaged in some sort of a conversation, were Noel and Evan Larson.

She felt an icy chill shimmy up and down her spine.

Twins, the Larsons were businessmen with extensive real estate holdings who used both their good looks and highly developed charm to get people to trust them. Word had it from Finn and some of her other law enforcement relatives that the Larsons were dangerous and building a criminal empire involving drugs, guns, high-stakes theft and money laundering.

But to Serena, Noel and Evan Larson would always be the creepy duo who had duped her in high school. Back then, she had briefly dated Evan—up until the time Noel had decided to switch places with his twin. Posing as Evan, he'd tried to pressure her into going further with him than she was willing to go. Upset, Serena summarily dumped Evan only to be told by him that it was his twin who had tried to get her into bed.

Stunned, Serena was furious that he had so cavalierly passed her off to his twin without her consent and Evan had reciprocated by being angry with her because she hadn't been able to tell the difference between him and his twin immediately. He wound up reviling her and calling her a number of names, including a dumb bitch. It was the last time they ever exchanged any words.

From that time on, Serena steered clear of both the twins, wanting nothing to do with either of them because of the deception and because of the demeaning way they had acted toward her.

In a nutshell, the Larsons scared her. They had scared her then and they scared her now, she realized as she rode up toward her brother. Even so, she felt that Anders needed backup.

She reached her brother just as Evan and Noel rode away.

Just as well, Serena thought. The very thought of being anywhere near the Larsons or having to talk to either one of them, left a really horrible taste in her mouth.

The only thing worse was allowing the duo to roam free on the Double C Ranch. She wanted them gone from the family property.

"What did they want?" she asked Anders the moment she reached her brother.

Anders frowned, intently watching the twins as the duo rode away. "Exactly what I asked them— after I told those two that they were trespassing on private property."

"And what was their answer?" Serena had no idea what to expect when it came to those two.

"Noel, at least that was who he said he was," Anders said, "told me they didn't 'realize' that they were trespassing. According to Noel, they were just out here 'admiring the gorgeous land' and they were thinking of buying a ranch themselves. They wanted to know if there were any ranches for sale in the area and asked a bunch of general questions about ranching. Seemed innocent enough, I suppose."

She didn't believe a word of it. There was something underhanded going on, she just didn't know what it was yet.

"They're not," Serena assured her brother with feeling. "Everything the Larsons do or say has some kind of hidden agenda, some kind of underhanded motive. A hundred and fifty years ago those two would have been snake oil salesmen—or made a living as gun runners to the Native population." She felt her stomach turning every time she thought of the twin brothers. "I wouldn't trust either one of them any farther than I could throw them," she told Anders. "From where I was, it looked like those two were riding around, casing the Double C Ranch."

Anders laughed shortly. "They know better than that."

"No, they don't," Serena maintained. "If you ask me, I think we should be on our guard." But waiting for something to happen would put the ranch's hands on edge, she thought. Something more specific was needed. "I think that we should also call Finn so his people will be on alert."

Anders shrugged. She knew he didn't care for the implication. He didn't like the idea of having to go running to his older brother. "I can take care of the ranch."

She was quick to correct the misunderstanding and set his mind at ease. "Nobody's saying that you can't take care of the ranch, Anders. But these guys *are* dangerous," Serena reminded him. "I get a sick feeling in the pit of my stomach just knowing that they're out there, poking around."

Anders sighed. "Okay, if it makes you feel any better, call Finn and tell him the Larsons were out here, looking like they were getting the lay of the land." He paused, his gaze on his sister. "I don't like the Larson twins any more than you do, Serena, but until they do something wrong that can be proved in a court of law, I don't think there's all that much Finn and his people can do about it."

One step at a time, Serena thought. "We can leave that up to Finn. At least we can get him started by giving him the information. Meanwhile," Serena said, as she leaned over in her saddle, patting the hilt of her rifle, "I'm keeping my rifle loaded—just in case."

Turning her mare around, Serena headed back to the stables. She left Nighthawk with one of the stable hands. It wasn't something she would normally do— she liked looking after and caring for her own horse, and that included unsaddling the mare and grooming her—but right now, she felt this sense of urgency nagging at her. She wanted to call Finn and tell him about finding the Larsons on the family ranch.

The call to the station proved frustrating. The person manning the front desk told her that Finn was out on a call. Before she knew it, she was being switched to someone else.

And then a deep voice was in her ear, saying, "Gage. What can I do for you?"

There were a number of Gages working in the police station. The odds of getting Carson were small. And yet, she just *knew* it was him.

Hoping against hope that she was wrong, she asked, "Carson?"

"Yes," the rumbling voice said gruffly.

Oh great, just the person I wanted to have talk down to me, she thought, annoyed. But she had a feeling that it was Carson or no one and she disliked having the Larson twins casing her ranch more than she disliked talking to the K-9 detective, so she decided to remain on the line.

"Detective Gage," she said, addressing him formally, "this is Serena Colton."

The detective's voice was just as cold as hers was. "Hello, Miss Colton. Did you think of something else you forgot to tell me?"

She almost hung up on him then. His tone of voice annoyed her. He sounded judgmental. But then maybe she was reading something into it, Serena told herself, struggling to remain fair. She decided to give him another chance.

"No," she told Carson, "I didn't forget anything. I just thought you might be interested in knowing that the Larson brothers were just out here, riding around the Double C. I swear they were taking measure of the ranch like a tailor measuring someone for a suit."

Mention of the Larsons had Carson immediately sitting up, alert.

"The Larsons," he repeated, digesting what she'd just said. "Anyone in your family have any reason to have dealings with those two?"

"No one in my family deals with vermin," Serena informed him coldly.

"Just checking," he told her. "I meant no offense," he added, taking her tone of voice into account.

And then she suddenly remembered something that had slipped her mind until just now.

"For the record, you might want to look into the dealings that your brother had with them," she told Carson. "Demi mentioned something about that to me one of the last times I saw her," Serena added.

"My brother? Dorian?" he asked.

Dorian, younger than he was by six years, was a bounty hunter, and this last year, Dorian had been Demi's chief competitor.

"No," Serena answered. She paused for a moment for effect before telling him, "Bo."

"What?" He was certain that he had to have heard her wrong.

Serena gave him all the information she had. "Demi told me that Bo sold the Larsons two of his German shepherds and that the Larsons paid one of the trainers at the K-9 center a lot of money on the down low to cross-train the dogs to attack. They were also trained to protect and detect."

"To detect what?" Carson wanted to know. He wasn't exactly happy about this piece of information. Bo had never said anything about selling two of his dogs to the Larsons.

What had Bo been thinking, doing business with the likes of the Larsons? He had to have known that they were under investigation. The twins' unsavory dealings weren't exactly a secret.

"Sorry," Serena answered. "I have no idea. That's something you're going to have to ask the Larsons."

He fully intended to, Carson thought. It was funny how the investigation into his brother's murder was making him come full circle, back to the investigation he'd been focused on prior to Bo's murder.

Were those two would-be crime kingpins somehow responsible for Bo's death? This case was getting more and more complicated.

"Thanks for bringing this to my attention," he told Serena, feeling that he owed her something, especially after the way he'd talked down to her.

It wasn't his attention she'd been after, Serena thought. "To be honest, I was trying to reach Finn to tell him about this," she said, not wanting any credit she didn't have coming to her.

The woman certainly made it difficult to give her a compliment, Carson thought. "Yeah, well, thanks anyway," he said just before he hung up the landline.

The Larson brothers, Carson thought, getting up from his desk. Maybe he was going to get to nail these bastards in this lifetime after all.

Dozing next to Carson's desk, Justice was instantly alert the second Carson had pushed back his chair. The German shepherd scrambled to his feet, ready to go wherever his two-footed partner went.

"I don't want you taking a bite out of either one of these slime-buckets," Carson warned as he secured the dog's leash onto his collar. "Not until *after* we have the goods on them. We got a deal, Justice?"

The German shepherd barked in response and Carson nodded his head as if they had just struck a bargain. "Deal," he echoed.

Noel and Evan Larson had a suite of impressive, swanky offices located downtown. Initially, the office had housed a real estate business. The story was that their business "grew," necessitating more space until their so-called "holdings" caused them to take over the rest of the building.

Decorated to create envy in the eye of the beholder, Carson found that the suite of offices looked to be pretentious. He himself had always favored clean, simple lines. In his home and in his partner, he thought, glancing over at Justice.

Walking into the Larsons' offices, he didn't bother waiting for the administrative assistant sitting at the front desk to announce him. Instead, he walked right past her into the inner suite and announced himself.

One step behind him, the administrative assistant looked at her bosses in obvious distress. "I'm sorry, sirs. He got away from me."

"That's all right, Bailey Jean," Noel said. "We'll

take it from here." He waved the woman back to the front desk.

Carson held up his ID for the two brothers to view. "Detective Gage," he told the duo, although he knew that they were well aware of who he was. "I'd like to have a word with you if I could."

He was sure the look on his face told the two men that this wasn't a request but a flat-out order. Knowing that they liked playing the game, he wasn't expecting any resistance from either one.

"Sure thing, Detective," Evan said, standing next to his twin. "You mind leaving that mutt outside? Like in your car?" he stressed. It was obvious that he felt uncomfortable around the German shepherd.

Carson was not about to leave the dog anywhere but at his side. Having the animal there evened the odds in his opinion.

"This is Justice. My partner," he told the duo. "Justice goes where I go."

"Rather simplistic, don't you think, Detective?" Noel asked with a smirk.

Identical in every way when it came to their appearance, Noel had always been the one everyone regarded as the ringleader, and he had taken the lead now, as was his habit.

"No, I don't," Carson answered flatly. He made it clear that no matter what their unspoken criminal connections were, he was not intimidated. "Can we get on with this, gentlemen?"

"We'll answer any question you have, Detective," Noel said in a friendly, easygoing manner. He glanced in his brother's direction. In contrast to Noel, Evan appeared to be as stiff as a board. "Sit, Evan," Noel told his twin. "You're making the detective's dog nervous."

Evan hadn't taken his eyes off Justice since the dog had walked into the office. Carson saw that there was a thin line of perspiration all along the quiet twin's upper lip.

"The dog's making *me* nervous," Evan retorted.

"Don't mind Evan," Noel told Carson. "My brother doesn't get along well with dogs. Or, on occasion, people," he added as a snide aside. "Now, what is it that we can do for you, Detective?"

For now, Carson just wanted a couple of questions answered. "Did you buy two German shepherds from my brother?" Carson asked.

"Such a shame what happened to Bo," Noel said as if talking about the weather. "But to answer your question, as a matter of fact, we did."

"Why?"

Noel smiled at him. "I really don't see how that's any business of yours, Detective."

"This is a murder investigation," Carson informed him in an unemotional voice. "*Everything's* my business."

"All right," Noel replied in an accommodating tone. "We keep a large amount of cash in our safe for instant sales. We need the dogs to guard the place, keep people from trying to break in and help themselves to it. The dogs, Hans and Fisher," he said, making the two sound more like favored employees rather than guard dogs, "were trained specifically to guard the safe." Noel's grin widened. "I can give you a little demonstration if you'd like."

He had no desire to watch a demonstration, not with Justice at his side. If the other dogs showed any sign of aggression, too much could go wrong.

"No, for now your explanation is good enough for me," he told Noel. Although he couldn't help wondering why the dogs had been purchased, given Evan's obvious fear of German shepherds. Something wasn't adding up.

"Great. Anything else?" Noel asked, making it sound as if he had all the time in the world to spare for the detective.

"Yes." He waited a moment before continuing. "Serena Colton said she saw you riding around on her property earlier. Mind telling me why?"

"Don't mind at all," Noel said. "We're thinking of buying a ranch for ourselves and just wanted to take a look at one of the more successful ranches in the area." Noel flashed two rows of perfect teeth at him.

"And that's it?"

"That's it," Noel told him, "Except I think that we must have spooked her. Didn't mean to, of course. Anything else?" he asked.

"Not right now," Carson answered. Holding

firmly on to Justice's leash, he nodded at the two brothers and took his leave.

"Well, if you think of anything, you know where to find us," Noel called after him cheerfully.

I sure as hell do, Carson thought, walking out.

Chapter 8

As he drove back to the police station, Carson went over the interview he had just conducted several times in his mind just in case he'd missed something.

Without a doubt, Noel and Evan Larson had to be the friendliest, seemingly accommodating cold-blooded criminals he'd ever had the misfortune of dealing with—and he didn't believe a single word that had come out of either one of their mouths.

There was something about the so-called charming duo, something he couldn't put his finger on just yet, but if the Larsons swore on a stack of bibles that something was true, he was more than willing to go out of his way to find the evidence that proved that it was false, because as sure as night followed day, it was.

He didn't think the two were capable of telling the truth if their very lives depended on it.

"I suppose that feeling that way doesn't exactly make me impartial, does it, Justice?" Carson asked, addressing the question to the German shepherd riding beside him. "Maybe the problem is that there're too many people willing to give those two a free pass. Too many people trying to get on their good side because they think that ingratiating themselves to the Larsons might get them to be part of their cushy world."

The real problem in this matter, Carson decided, was that he had no idea if what the Larsons were involved in had anything to do with Bo's death at all or if the two were mutually exclusive of one another. What he did know was that he wanted to find Bo's killer *and* he wanted to put the Larson brothers behind bars.

But that very possibly could be two very separate things.

Focus, he ordered himself. *Focus*.

He needed to find Bo's killer and then he could get back to the business of putting the Larsons behind bars, where they belonged.

One step at a time.

Finding Bo's killer brought him back to trying to find Demi. The woman wasn't exactly a shrinking violet in any sense of the term and she just couldn't have disappeared into thin air.

Someone had to have seen her, talked with her, *something*.

Determined to locate the bounty hunter and confront her with the additional evidence they'd found to see how she explained her way out of that, Carson decided to go back to the beginning and question some of the people Demi had interacted with. That would help him piece together her timeline for the day that Bo was murdered.

He hadn't managed to even get his seat warm at the station before one of the other K-9 cops held their landline receiver up in the air, calling out to get his attention.

"Hey, Gage, someone's asking to talk to you. Says it's about that missing redheaded bounty hunter," Joe Walker called out.

He'd already got a few crank calls, as well as a couple from people just looking for information about the investigation. These days, every third person with access to a computer fancied themselves a journalist.

He made no effort to pick up the phone. "Who is it?" Carson wanted to know.

"They won't say," Walker said. "Just want to talk to you. Line three," he prompted, wiggling the receiver.

With a sigh, Carson picked up his receiver and punched Line Three. "Gage," he announced.

"Carson Gage?" the raspy voice on the other end asked.

It was someone trying to disguise their voice and doing a very obvious job of it, Carson thought impatiently. He didn't have time for this. "Yes. Who am I talking to?"

"My name doesn't matter," the voice on the other end said. Carson was about to hang up when he heard the voice say, "All you need to know is that I work at the Double C Ranch and I just saw Demi Colton running from one of the barns. The one where the studio apartments are kept. You know, the ones the ranch hands live in."

He was a born skeptic. Still, he stayed on the line. "You just saw her?" Caron questioned.

"Less than fifteen minutes ago," the voice told him. Then, as if reading his mind, the caller said, "Look, you can believe me or not, but I saw what I saw and I heard you were looking for that Colton woman so I'm calling it in. Do what you want with it."

"What did you say your name was again?" Carson asked, trying to get the caller to slip up.

"I didn't."

The line went dead.

He dropped the receiver into its cradle. The call could have very well just been a hoax, someone trying to get him to chase his tail for the sheer perverse fun of it.

But on the other hand, Carson felt that he couldn't afford to ignore it, either. He needed to check out this latest so-called "tip."

"I'm going back to the Double C Ranch," Carson told the detective sitting closest to him just in case the chief came looking for him.

Immersed in a report he was wading through on his desk, Emilio Sanchez raised an inquisitive eyebrow. "Got something?"

"I sure as hell hope so," was all Carson was willing to share at the moment as he walked out of the squad room. Justice quickly followed him out.

Serena was just coming out of the stables, talking to one of the horse trainers who worked for her when she saw Carson driving up. Her first thought was that the detective was coming back because he had something to tell her about the Larsons.

"I'll talk to you later, Juan," she said to the trainer. With her eyes riveted on Carson's approaching vehicle, she hurried toward it.

She saw that, despite the cold weather, the window on his side was partially down. "I didn't expect you to be back so soon," Serena told him as she walked up to the driver's side.

"That makes two of us," Carson answered. He turned off the ignition.

Was he waiting for her to pry the information out of him? "So? What did you find out?" Serena asked impatiently.

The woman was standing right up against his door, inadvertently preventing him from opening it. Carson indicated the door with his eyes, waiting.

Annoyance creasing her forehead, Serena stepped back, allowing him to open the door and get out. Justice was right behind him and came bounding out of the driver's side.

If she thought he was here to fill her in on how his meeting with the Larsons went, she was in for a big surprise, Carson thought.

"I found out that you weren't being entirely truthful with me," he said, thinking of the call he'd taken about Demi's sighting. The call that was responsible for his being here.

Her eyes narrowed to brown slits as she glared at Carson. "What are you talking about? What did those lying snakes tell you?"

What was she talking about? "Come again?"

She bit back the urge to tell him to keep up. "The Larson brothers. What delusional story did they try to sell you?"

"The Larsons?" he echoed. Why would his saying that she hadn't been entirely truthful make her think of the Larsons? Was there a reason she'd pointed him in their direction?

Was the detective deliberately playing dumb? She

was beginning to think that the German shepherd was the smart one of the pair.

"Yes, the Larsons," she said evenly. "Didn't you come back to tell me how your meeting with them went?"

Well, she obviously thought a lot of herself, Carson thought, irritated. "No. I'm here because someone from the Double C just called the police station to say that they saw Demi, not fifteen minutes ago, running from one of the studio apartments you have for the ranch hands." He pinned her with a very cold look. "You lied to me, Ms. Colton."

Serena's temper flared. "I *didn't* lie to you and seeing as how you keep insulting my integrity, why don't we just drop the polite 'Ms. Colton' act, shall we?" she snapped.

Maintaining a respectful air came naturally to him, but given the situation, it was apparently lost on this woman.

"Fine by me, *Serena*." He deliberately enunciated her name.

"Well, none of this is 'fine by me,'" Serena retorted. "And doesn't it strike you as odd that someone who has a perfectly reliable vehicle the way, I'm sure you know, that Demi does is always being spotted 'running' around?" She blew out a breath trying to tamp down her temper. "This is all getting very tiresome, Carson," she said, calling him by his first name and saying it through clenched teeth. "Please leave."

He had no intention of doing anything of the sort. "Sorry, I can't do that. Not until I've searched the barns and surrounding area for Demi."

Serena fisted her hands at her waist, ready to go toe-to-toe with him. "And if I tell you that you can't?" she challenged.

Carson took a folded piece of paper out of his pocket, opened it and held it up for her to look at. "This warrant says I can."

Fuming, Serena unceremoniously took the warrant from him and scanned it.

"Meet with your approval?" he asked when she folded the paper and handed it back to him.

"No," Serena snapped. None of this met with her approval. "But it is a warrant," she conceded. "So I guess I can't stop you. But you're wasting your time," she informed him. "Demi's still not here. Whoever called you is sending you on a wild-goose chase. So—"

Serena stopped talking suddenly, her head whipping around to look over her shoulder toward something she thought she heard.

Justice was straining at his leash. Obviously whatever it was, the dog had heard it, too, so this wasn't just an act on Serena's part, he thought.

"What?" he asked her in a hushed voice.

But she didn't answer him. Instead Serena hurried around the side of what had initially been one of the barns on the original ranch, before the ranch had been renovated and expanded.

He read Serena's body language. Something definitely had the horse breeder going, he thought as he and Justice followed her.

He was fairly certain that she was not attempting to lead them to corner Demi, but there was no arguing that Serena was after someone.

Someone she apparently was keenly interested in confronting.

Carson caught her by the arm before she got away from him. When she tried to pull free, he just tightened his hold. Serena glared at him.

"Who are you trying to corral?" he wanted to know.

"My sister," she hissed, annoyed that he was intervening and getting in her way.

Serena tried to pull free again with the same results. The only way this ape was going to let go of her was if she answered his question. So, unwillingly, she did.

"I think the Larsons are trying to get their hooks into Valeria." The second he released her, she made her way around the barn and looked into the first window she could. "She's impressionable and flighty and," she continued, moving to the next window, "with your brother!"

Rapping her knuckles against the window to get

their attention, she didn't stop until the two people on the bed finally separated and looked her way.

The two had been so completely wrapped around one another that had it not been for the different colors of their clothing, it would have been hard to distinguish where all their separate limbs began and ended.

Trying the door, Serena found it unlocked and stormed in. Carson followed behind her just as Justice got past him and got in between the two younger people.

"Vincent?" Carson cried. The last person he expected to find in this compromising position with a Colton was his youngest brother.

Startled at being discovered as well as suddenly having a German shepherd getting in between them and wagging his tail in a display of friendly recognition, Valeria and Vincent instantly pulled apart and were up on their feet.

The two looked somewhat disheveled, not to mention disoriented and embarrassed. At least Vincent was. The nineteen-year-old mechanic had got a job working part-time on the Double C, fixing not just some of the cars but also other, larger mechanical devices on the ranch.

He was not, Carson thought, supposed to be giving the boss's daughter the same sort of close scrutiny he gave the vehicles he repaired.

Vincent gulped and finally found his tongue. "Carson, what are you doing here?"

"Thinking about spraying water on the two of you," Carson answered, frowning.

Incensed, Valeria immediately spoke up, turning her anger on her sister. "Hey, you have no right to be spying on us. We're both over eighteen and we can do whatever we want," she cried.

Serena didn't see it that way. "Are you out of your mind?" Serena demanded. "You know the way Dad feels about Vincent's father, how he feels about the whole Gage family," she emphasized. "If he catches the two of you going at it like two rabbits in heat, he'll string Vincent up without a second thought."

Valeria raised her chin, ready to protect this precious romance she was involved in. "He'd have to go through me to do it!" she declared defiantly, her eyes blazing.

"Don't think for a minute that he won't," Serena retorted. "Nothing is more important to that man than the ideas of family honor—and Dad puts that 'honor' above all of us."

Valeria became angrier if that was possible. "I don't care what's important to *him*," she insisted. "Vincent is important to me," she said, reaching for his hand.

The youngest of the Gage clan closed his hand around hers.

"And you don't have to worry and carry on about

honor," Valeria continued. "Vincent and I are getting married on Christmas Eve." She shared a smile with him before turning back toward her sister and Vincent's big brother. "That happens to be Vincent's birthday and it's mine, too," she told them. "That makes the date doubly special. We'll both be turning twenty that day," she added as if that fact somehow added weight to what they were planning.

Ignoring the man next to her, Serena made a valiant attempt to talk some sense into her sister. "Valeria, you're both too young to make such a life-altering decision at this stage."

"For once," Carson interjected, "I agree with Serena."

Valeria tossed her head and looked at her sister, totally ignoring the detective. This was between her sister and her. "Seems to me that a woman with a baby and no husband shouldn't be lecturing us on what we should or shouldn't do," she said dismissively.

Carson saw the flash of hurt in Serena's eyes. No one was more surprised than he was when he felt something protective stir within him.

"Tossing insults at your sister," he told Valeria coldly, "doesn't change the fact that what you are contemplating doing is foolhardy, and it's opening the two of you up to a real flood of anger—coming at you from both families."

"But, Carson, it's a really stupid feud," Vincent protested.

"I'm not arguing that," Carson granted. "It's beyond stupid. Half the members of both families can't even remember how the whole damn thing got started or what it's even about. Hell, I'm not even sure. Near as I can tell, it was something about land issues that had our grandfathers at each other's throats, or so the story goes according to our father," he said, nodding at Vincent. "But it doesn't matter how it got started. What matters is that it's still going on and if you two go through with what you're planning, that damn feud is probably going to escalate. So, if I were you two," Carson said, looking from one to the other, "I'd hold off getting married for a while."

"Well, you're not us," Vincent told his brother, putting a protective arm around Valeria as if to signify that it was the two of them against the world if that's what it took for them to get married.

Valeria looked at Carson. "And just how long is 'a while'?" she demanded hotly. She had her hand on her hip, the very picture of a woman who was not about to change her mind no matter what.

"As long as it takes to get our families to come around," Serena answered. She knew that was vague, but there was no way to put a timetable on getting the two families to reconcile.

Valeria shook her head. The answer was unacceptable.

"Sorry, can't wait that long. I'll be an old lady by the time that happens. You want them to change their minds?" Valeria laid down a challenge. "You see if you can do it before Christmas Eve," she told her sister. "But one way or another, Vincent and I are getting married."

Taking Vincent's hand again, she laced her fingers through his and said, "Let's get out of here, Vincent. It's way too stuffy for me."

"Yeah," Vincent agreed. The youngest Gage brother only had eyes for Valeria and gave every indication that he would follow her to the ends of the earth if need be. "Me, too."

Chapter 9

Feeling incensed as she watched her sister and Vincent walk away, most likely to find another place where they could be alone, Serena swung around and directed her anger at the K-9 detective who was still standing next to her.

Her eyes were blazing as she demanded, "Are you just going to let them go like that?"

"Can't arrest them for being in love," Carson told her. He was almost amused by the fiery display he'd just witnessed, but he knew better than to let Serena suspect that. "And no matter what your father or my father think about the other person's family, there are no laws being broken here." He could see that Serena was far from satisfied with his answer. "Just what is it that you want me to do?"

Serena threw her hands up, angry and exasperated. "I don't know," she cried, walking back around to the front of the building. *"Something!"*

"I am doing something," Carson shot back. "I'm trying to find the person who killed my brother," he reminded Serena.

From what she could see, all he was doing was spinning his wheels, poking around on her ranch. "Well, you're not going to find that person here, and you're not going to find Demi here, either," she told him for what felt like the umpteenth time, knowing that no matter what he said, her cousin was still the person he was looking for.

"If you don't mind, I'd like to check that out for myself," Carson told her.

"Yes, I do mind," she retorted angrily. "I mind this constant invasion of our privacy that you've taken upon yourself to commit by repeatedly coming here and—"

As she was railing at him, out of the corner of his eye he saw Justice suddenly becoming alert. Rather than the canine fixing his attention on Serena and the loud dressing-down she was giving him, the German shepherd seemed to be looking over toward another one of the barns that contained more of the hands' living quarters.

At this time of day, the quarters should have been

empty. Even so, he intended to search them on the outside chance that this was where Demi was hiding.

Something had got the highly trained canine's attention. Was it Demi? Had she come here in her desperation only to have one of the hands see her and subsequently put in a call to the station? Was she hiding here somewhere?

"What is it, Justice? What do you—"

He got no further with his question.

The bone-chilling crack of a gun—a rifle by the sound of it—being discharged suddenly shattered the atmosphere. Almost simultaneously, a bullet whizzed by them, so close that he could almost feel it disturb the air.

Instinct took over. Carson threw himself on Serena, covering her with his body as he got her behind what had to be Valeria's car. The one Vincent was supposed to be working on.

Startled, Serena couldn't speak for a moment because the air had been knocked out of her. The next second, she demanded, "What do you think you're doing?"

"Trying to save your life, damn it," Carson snapped.

Justice broke into a run and whizzed by him, heading straight for the barn. The main door was open.

Pulling out his sidearm, Carson ordered Serena, "Stay down," and took off after his K-9 partner.

"The hell I will," Serena retorted.

Scrambling up to her feet, she cursed the fact that

it took her a second to steady herself. And then she quickly followed in their wake.

Reaching the barn, Carson began to move from one uniform room to another. Whoever had fired at them had done so from one of the windows facing the other barn. They were also gone.

Cursing under his breath, he kept his gun drawn as he scanned the area.

Justice was barking in what could only be termed a display of frustration. The dog was expressing himself, Carson thought, for both of them.

When he heard a noise behind him, Carson whirled around, his weapon cocked and ready to fire. He could feel his heart slam against his chest when he realized it was Serena and that he had come within a hair's breadth of shooting her.

"Damn it, woman," he said, resetting the trigger, "I told you to stay put. I could have killed you."

Her eyes met his. There was still fire in hers. "The feeling's mutual," she informed him.

The sudden, unexpected feel of his body pressing against hers like that had brought back all sorts of sensations and emotions, which were running rampant through her. She welcomed none of them. Even so, her body refused to stop throbbing and vibrating and it totally unnerved her.

Despite her agitation and the anger it created, Serena immediately recognized the feeling for what it was. She had been aroused.

Was aroused. And damn it, she didn't want to be. The last time she'd felt that way, nine months later she was giving birth to a baby.

Giving birth and vowing that she was never, *ever* going to allow herself to get into this sort of predicament again. And, until just a few minutes ago, she was completely certain that she never would. She'd been positive that she had sworn off men for the rest of her life, dedicating herself to her daughter and to her job on the Double C.

And now, after a year's hiatus, her body was practically begging her to abandon limbo and feel like a woman again. Begging her to revisit that glorious feeling of having every single inch of her body tingle because she was responding to a man's touch.

Carson stared at her in confusion. What the hell was she talking about? "I was talking about you sneaking up on me like that."

"I didn't sneak," Serena declared defensively, desperately trying to regain control over herself. "This is my family's ranch, and I've got a right to know what's going on."

"Of all the harebrain— You want to know what's going on?" he shouted at her. "Someone just shot at you, Serena. *That's* what's going on. And if I hadn't been there just now, they might have killed you!" he exclaimed. "You're welcome!" he yelled at her when she said nothing in response.

He'd knocked her down and almost given her a

concussion, the big oaf! Serena was the picture of fury as she retorted, "I didn't say thank you."

"I can't help it if you have no manners," Carson shot back. Fed up, he began to storm away.

She wasn't about to stand for him turning his back on her like this. "Now, you just wait a damn minute!" Serena exclaimed, grabbing hold of his shoulder and attempting to pull Carson around to face her.

His emotions were running at a fever pitch and not just because someone had discharged a rifle, narrowly missing them. If he was being honest with himself, something had been stirred up when he had first seen Serena standing at the top of the landing with her baby in her arms. Seeing her had unearthed something, keenly digging into his mind and soul. Reminding him of what he had lost before he had ever been allowed to have it.

It had given him a reason to shut Serena Colton out.

But for some perverse reason, it had also given him a reason to want this woman. Want this woman the way he hadn't wanted any other, not since he'd lost Lisa. All the while, as he had been involved in the search for his brother's killer, this feeling had been messing with his mind.

Messing with it to such a degree that he'd allowed himself to entertain irrational thoughts.

Like pulling Serena into his arms and sealing his mouth to hers so he could still the needs that insisted on multiplying within him. That insisted on taunting him and giving him no peace.

Carson came perilously close to going with that desire. And he would have if a livid Anders Colton hadn't picked that exact moment to all but burst onto the scene.

"What the hell is going on here?" Anders demanded as he came upon his sister and the detective.

For a split second both Serena and Carson shared a single thought. That Anders's question was about what had come very close to happening between them—Serena had felt the pull, too—and not about the gunshot that had resounded loud enough for anyone close by to hear.

Serena drew in a deep breath, trying valiantly to still her pounding heart and get control over her all but runaway pulse.

"What?" she asked.

"The gunshot," Anders shouted. His expression demanded to know if she had gone deaf. "I just heard a gunshot," the foremen cried angrily. "What the hell is going on here?"

By now, some of ranch hands had also come running over as well, as had Valeria and Vincent.

At the sight of the two younger people, surprise and then anger crossed the Double C foreman's face.

"What are you doing with my sister?" he demanded, glaring at Vincent. He forgot all about the gunshot as the thought of the mechanic's questionable behavior came to the foreground.

"Later," Carson told Serena's brother authoritatively. "Right now, you've got bigger problems than Romeo and Juliet over there," he said. "Someone just took a shot at Serena." Serena had to be the target, he thought. Had the shooter been after him, there had been plenty of opportunities to shoot at him prior to now.

"Serena?" Dumbfounded, Anders's attention shifted to her. She looked none the worse for wear. Was the detective lying to him? "Why would anyone shoot at Serena?"

"Why does anyone shoot at someone?" Carson countered, exasperated.

Realizing that Carson was telling him the truth, Anders put his hands on Serena's shoulders as he looked his sister over closely. His voice was filled with concern as he asked, "Are you hurt?"

"Just slightly bruised," she answered. "Detective Gage decided he was bulletproof and took it upon himself to act as my human shield."

Anders flushed, torn between being grateful and his natural feelings of resentment when it came to anyone who belonged to the Gage family.

Feeling that he should offer the detective an apology, he began, "Look, if I just came off sounding like an idiot—"

"Save it," Carson said, waving away what sounded

as if it was shaping up to be a very awkward apology. "The first order of business until I can find this shooter is to pack up your family and get them off the ranch and someplace safe."

Anders was in total agreement with the detective. "I'll have my parents and sisters move into the hotel in town until this blows over."

"Wouldn't be a bad idea for you to go, too," Carson told him.

But here they had a parting of the ways when it came to agreement. Everyone on the ranch couldn't just leave. The ranch had to continue being productive.

"I'm the ranch foreman," Anders told him. "I'm responsible for the staff on the Double C. I'm not about to leave them, especially not when there's some crazy shooter loose."

Carson sighed. "Look, I can't make you go—" he began.

"No, you can't," Anders agreed, interrupting the detective.

"And that goes for me, too," Serena informed him, speaking up.

Carson whirled around to face her. This was getting out of hand. "You were the one who was just shot at," he reminded her.

"How do you know?" she challenged, surprising him. "Maybe whoever it was that was shooting just now was aiming at you."

That was ridiculous. She was grasping at straws, pulling thin arguments out of the air. "If that's the case, they would have had plenty of opportunity to shoot at me. They didn't have to wait until I came here to the ranch. You were the target," he insisted.

Be that as it may, she was not about to have Carson tell her what to do. "If that's the case, I'm a big girl, and I can decide whether I stay or go." She raised her chin, sticking it out as a way of asserting herself. "And I've decided to stay."

Stubborn woman! All he could do was block any of her senseless moves.

"I can't let you do that."

Who the hell did this man think he was? "You have nothing to say about it," she informed Carson. "Besides, whoever just shot at us," she said, deliberately underscoring the word *us*, "can and *will* come after us, no matter where we are. There's no point in me running," she argued. "The ranch has a couple of safe rooms inside the mansion. As a last resort, if it comes down to that, I can hide in one of them," she said, her tone clearly declaring that it was the end of the debate as far as she was concerned.

Caught completely off guard, Carson looked at the foreman. This was the first time he'd heard that there were safe rooms within the sprawling mansion.

"Is this true?" he asked Anders. "The mansion has safe rooms in it?"

"Of course it's true," Serena retorted, speaking

up because she was annoyed that the detective had asked her brother instead of her. "There's no reason for me to lie about that."

"No," Carson agreed. "There isn't." He processed this new piece of information, then turned toward Anders. "I want to see those safe rooms."

"Why?" Serena wanted to know, once again interrupting. "You want to inspect them to see if they live up to your high standards?" she mocked.

She felt as if Carson was determined to block her at every turn. She certainly didn't like him questioning her every move the way he did.

Maybe, if she hadn't reacted to him the way she had when he'd thrown himself over her, she wouldn't feel anywhere nearly as combative as she did. She didn't know, but now was not the time for her to suddenly start questioning and doubting herself.

"No," Carson answered Serena. "I want to see if Demi's in either one of them. If you ask me, it sounds like a really logical place for her to be holed up," he told Serena.

"She doesn't know a thing about them," Serena informed him, annoyed that she had essentially been forced to share this secret with the likes of him. "Nobody does. Only family members do. That means," she told him, clenching her teeth, "that Demi's not *there*. Give it up, Detective."

"You won't mind if I satisfy my curiosity, do you?" he asked sarcastically.

"As a matter of fact, I do," she informed him coldly. "And I'm not taking you to them."

"If you have nothing to hide, there's no reason not to take me to those safe rooms," he said, prepared to go toe-to-toe with her—or have a judge sort it out after she spent a night in lockup.

"The reason is I don't want to," Serena informed him stubbornly.

"Not good enough," he said, taking out the warrant again and holding it up to her.

"That doesn't say you can search the safe rooms," she retorted.

"It says," he answered, emphasizing each word, "I can search the immediate premises—so unless the safe rooms are hovering somewhere above the ranch," his voice dripped with sarcasm, "they're considered to be part of the premises."

Valeria uttered a frustrated, guttural sound as she lost her patience. "Oh, take him to go see them, Serena. We're not going to get rid of him or his dog otherwise," she insisted.

"You're getting rid of him because you're going to be staying at the hotel with Mom and Dad," Serena reminded her sister.

Valeria drew herself up to her full height. "I am *not* going," she protested between clenched teeth.

"You're going, little sister, even if you have to be dragged there kicking and screaming," Anders informed her.

Angry, fuming and utterly frustrated, Valeria looked in Vincent's direction as her brother pulled her after him to the mansion. "I cannot *wait* to get married," she cried plaintively.

"Well, you're *not* married, and right now you're my responsibility," Anders informed her, maintaining a tight grip around her wrist as he continued on his way to the mansion.

Chapter 10

As he watched Valeria being dragged back to the mansion, Vincent turned toward Carson. He looked clearly concerned.

"Do you think she's really in any danger?" he asked his older brother.

Carson gave him his honest opinion without sugarcoating it. "I think all the Coltons here are in danger," he answered. "Which is why," he continued, looking in Serena's direction, "you and your baby should go with your parents and Valeria to stay at the hotel in Red Ridge."

Serena made a disparaging, dismissive noise. "Nice touch, Carson, having your baby brother play straight man for you like that, but I'm still not leaving the Double C."

Carson knew he was getting nowhere, but he still felt that he had to try.

"You're being unreasonable," he told Serena, struggling with his temper. "That shooter missed you last time. He—or she—might not the next time."

"There's not going to be a next time," Serena countered with a huff. "Because you are going to catch him—"

"Or her," Carson interjected pointedly.

She knew what he was doing. He was making it seem as if Demi had been the one who'd pulled the trigger. But that was absolutely ridiculous. There was no reason for the bounty hunter to have tried to shoot her. They had actually become friends, at least to some degree. With that in mind, Serena deliberately ignored the detective's interjection and went on talking.

"—like the county's paying you to do."

Carson shook his head, exasperated. The woman was being brave and damn foolhardy at the same time. "You never did have a lick of sense."

Serena flashed a wide smile at him. "Must be nice for you to be able to count on some things never changing," she told Carson sweetly.

He had a feeling that Serena could go on like this until the proverbial cows came home. But he didn't have time for that.

"I hope your brother's having more luck with your parents than I'm having with you," Carson told her as he headed straight for the mansion.

When he walked into the foyer, he was just in time to hear Serena's mother making her displeasure loudly known to one and all. Somehow, though he hadn't walked into the house until just now, Joanelle Colton was holding him *and* his family accountable for this newest inconvenient series of events in her life.

"You," Joanelle cried, sidestepping her daughter as if she didn't exist and making her way directly over to the detective. She stopped short abruptly, pulling back as if she wanted no part of her clothing to touch either Carson or his K-9 partner. "Just exactly *what* is the meaning of all this?" she demanded, furious. "Anders says we have to leave the ranch. Are you the one behind this proposed exodus?"

Aware that there were four pairs of Colton eyes fixed on him, Carson didn't rise to the bait.

Carson removed his hat before he spoke to Serena's mother. "I did suggest it, yes, ma'am. And it's for your own safety," he told her politely.

"Since when is a Gage worried about a Colton's safety?" Judson demanded, coming to his wife's side, his deep, booming voice all but echoing through the ground floor.

"Since I swore an oath to protect all the citizens of Red Ridge, Mr. Colton," Carson replied calmly.

He was determined that neither of the older

Coltons were going to rattle him. If worse came to worst, he could always turn the matter over to Finn and have *him* deal with his family.

Though she had her own issues with Carson, Serena knew that he was only trying to protect her family. She also knew firsthand how overbearing both her parents could get. Memories of their reactions when she was forced to come to them and tell them she was having a baby were very fresh in her mind. Neither parent had been easy to deal with or sympathetic, thinking only how this baby would ultimately reflect on them.

Angry bears were easier to reason with, she thought. Possibly also friendlier. Which was why, just for now, she threw her lot in with Carson.

"Someone shot at me, Dad," she said emphatically. "Detective Gage is just trying to get you to stay somewhere safe until he can catch whoever it is that's out there, using us for target practice."

By the look on the patriarch's face, this was the first he was hearing of this. Incensed, Judson turned on Anders.

"Is this true?" he demanded.

"Someone did take a shot in Serena's direction when she was out by one of the barns where the hands have their quarters." Anders relayed the incident as best he could, given he hadn't been there to see it for himself. He had arrived after the fact, only drawn by the sound of gunfire.

Joanelle gasped, her hand flying to her chest. Carson expected the woman to express concern about her daughter's welfare, or at least ask Serena if she was all right. However, Joanelle appeared horrified that this sort of thing had happened on her ranch—to her.

"I knew it! I knew something like this would happen when you allowed that dreadful girl to invade our home. She had no business setting foot on my ranch!" Joanelle cried. "That branch of the family is just poor trash, tainting everything they come in contact with and you can't expect anything better from them. How *could* you, Serena?"

Her mother's histrionics never ceased to amaze her. "This isn't Demi's fault, Mother," Serena insisted, annoyed.

"Huh! Well, it'll take more than you saying that to convince me," Joanelle declared, wrapping her arms around herself and in essence sealing herself off. "What sort of a woman makes her living by being a bounty hunter for heaven's sake?"

Serena was exceedingly tired of her mother's judgmental, condescending attitude. "A resourceful one would be my guess," Serena countered.

Frosty blue eyes glared at Serena. "That's not what *I* call it," Joanelle fired back.

Serena was aware of the expression on Carson's face. He looked as if he felt sorry for her. Her back went up. She wasn't about to put on a show for the detective's entertainment.

"Shouldn't you be packing for the hotel, Mother?" she pointed out.

Joanelle scowled, obviously insulted by the suggestion. "That's what I have the maid for," she answered haughtily.

Wanting her mother to leave the foyer, Serena rephrased the question. "Then shouldn't you be supervising Marion as she packs for you?"

Unable to argue with that, Joanelle regally turned on her heel and made her way up the spiral staircase. "Come, Valeria!"

There was no room for argument or resistance in her voice.

Uttering an unintelligible, guttural cry, a furious Valeria stomped up the stairs behind her mother.

Judson looked at Serena. "I'd expect Anders to stay and run the ranch, but you should come with us," he told her in a voice that was only mildly less authoritative than his wife's.

"The household staff is staying," Serena began but her father cut in before she could finish.

"Don't worry." He looked at his son. "Anders will make sure that they don't take anything in our absence," Judson told her.

Serena instantly took offense for the staff. She liked the hardworking people, and they were definitely a lot nicer and kinder than her parents were.

How like her father to think that the staff was only interested in stealing from him.

"I'm sure they won't," she immediately replied. "Because they're honest, not because someone is watching them. However, I have work to do with the horses. Anders can't see to that as well as to everything else. Don't worry, Dad, I'll be fine, but you need to take Mother and Valeria out of here," she insisted in case her father was having second thoughts about going to the hotel.

Although she felt she could handle any danger to herself, she did want her family to be safe. "Mother's high-strung. If she stays here, she'll see a gun aimed at her behind every post and tree and make your life a living hell, you know that," she stressed.

The expression on her father's face told Serena that Judson Colton was well aware of what his wife was capable of.

As the elder Colton appeared to be mulling over the situation, Carson spoke up. "I'll stay on the ranch to make sure nothing happens to your daughter or your granddaughter, sir," he volunteered.

Unable to bring himself to actually express his thanks to a Gage, Judson merely nodded curtly.

"I have to pack," he said, more to himself than to the detective or his daughter. With that, he went upstairs.

The second her father left the immediate area,

Serena swung around to confront Carson. "You'll do no such thing!"

She caught him off guard. "What is it that I won't do?" he wanted to know.

"Stay here. I don't need you playing bodyguard," she informed him.

Unfazed by her rejection, Carson told her, "Just think of it as your tax dollars at work."

This wasn't funny. "I don't want—"

He'd held his tongue long enough. Serena would try an angel's patience, and he was far from an angel. "What you want, or need, is of no concern to me, Serena," he informed her. "Someone took a shot at you. I aim to find out who it was and to keep it from happening again," Carson told her fiercely. "Now, if you don't mind, I need to see those safe rooms you mentioned earlier."

Serena blew out an angry breath. She'd just assumed that he'd forgotten about the rooms. "I thought we were past that."

"No," he answered, "we're not." Just like Justice when he was hot on a scent, Carson was not about to get distracted. "And the only way we're ever getting 'past that' is if I can find Demi and question her about how her necklace wound up under the tire of that car that was near my brother's body."

Feeling as if she was the only one in Demi's corner, Serena tried to come up with some sort of an explanation for the evidence.

"Maybe someone's trying to frame her." The moment she said it out loud, it sounded right to her. "Did you ever think of that?" Serena challenged.

"No, gosh, I never did. What an unusual thought," Carson said sarcastically. And then he changed his tone, becoming serious as he told her, "Of course I thought of that, but until I can talk to Demi again and get some facts straightened out, I'm not going to waste time investigating that theory. Not when everything else clearly points to her killing my brother. Am I making myself clear?" he all but growled at her.

Serena's eyes narrowed, shooting daggers at him as she struggled to hold on to her temper. "As transparent as glass."

"Good," he retorted with finality. "Now, then, just where are those safe rooms that you said were in your house?"

She was sorely tempted to tell him to go look for the safe rooms himself, but she didn't want to give Carson an excuse to go wandering around the mansion, possibly tearing things up on his own. Although she found that being around him really unsettled her, especially after Carson had thrown his body over her like that, Serena thought it best if she just showed him the two safe rooms herself.

"They're this way," she said, sweeping past Carson.

Her attention was riveted to the top of the stairs. The less she looked at him, Serena felt, the better. Carson was too damn good-looking and she knew all about good-looking men. They were as shallow as a puddle and only interested in their own self-satisfaction.

Been there, done that, she thought as she went up the stairs.

Finding himself unaccountably more amused than irritated, Carson walked behind her. He maintained a light grip on Justice's leash as he led the canine up with him.

Bringing the detective and his four-footed partner to the second floor, Serena made her way into her suite.

When she entered, she saw that the housekeeper was there, changing Lora. The woman appeared surprised to see her—and even more surprised to see the detective and Justice.

"Are you back, Miss Serena?" the woman asked, one hand on Lora to keep the baby from kicking. Lora's diaper was only half-on.

"Just passing through, Alma," Serena answered. "Detective Gage wants to take a look at something," she explained vaguely.

Carson scanned the area. He'd already been to her suite the other night. There'd been no sign of Demi at the time, except for that discarded sweater.

"Where's the room?" he wanted to know. She had just brought him over to her walk-in closet, but that certainly didn't qualify as a safe room, he thought. Was she trying to pull something on him?

"Right here," Serena answered.

Reaching in, she pressed a button just inside the closet entrance. As she did so, the back wall with all her neatly arranged shoes parted and moved aside, exposing another door. There was a keypad on the wall right next to it.

Serena positioned herself in front of the keypad so that he wasn't able to see which of the keys she pressed. When she finished, the door opened, exposing a room that was nothing short of huge. Carson judged that it took up the entire length of the floor.

In it was a king-size bed, a state-of-the-art kitchenette and all sorts of things that would make having to take refuge here anything but a hardship.

Carson looked around slowly, taking it all in. It was impressive. "My first place was one-third this size," he commented.

Serena didn't doubt it. "My father tends to go overboard," she answered. "And he thought that if it came to us having to actually use a safe room, we might all have to stay in here."

Carson nodded. "It certainly is big enough. Go for it, Justice," he told the dog as he released the animal. "Seek!"

But rather than take off, the German shepherd moved around the huge area slowly. Nothing had caught his attention.

The safe room was actually more than just a single room. There were a couple of smaller "rooms" attached to it. Justice went from one end of the space to another, but unlike when he had uncovered her sweater, he found no trace of Demi.

In the end, the dog came trotting back to him.

"Satisfied?" Serena asked the detective.

Instead of answering her questions, he said, "You said safe *rooms*."

Serena sighed. "So I did."

Resigned, she turned around and led the way out of that safe room and then her suite. She wordlessly proceeded to lead Carson to another wing of the mansion.

"How do you not get lost here?" Carson asked her as they went to the wing that faced the rear of the property.

"I use bread crumbs," she answered drolly, then immediately regretted it.

The sound of his laughter was way too sexy.

This safe room, like the other, turned out to be a room within a room. This one was hidden behind a floor-to-ceiling bookcase that housed a wealth of books as well as expensive knickknacks and memorabilia.

"It's here," she told him, entering another code on the keypad beside *that* door.

In Carson's estimation, the second room looked like a carbon copy of the first one, containing the same supplies, the same well-furnished distractions.

She stood off to one side, silently telling him he was free to search this room the way he had the other.

She felt that the sooner this was out of the way, the sooner Carson would leave and she could stop feeling as if she was having trouble breathing.

"Okay, Justice," Carson said, removing the canine's leash for a second time. "Go for it. Seek!"

Again the German shepherd moved about the large room and its connecting rooms as if there was a heavy dose of glue deposited in his veins.

Nothing seemed to pique the canine's interest, but the dog dutifully went around the entire area, sniffing, nudging items and in general taking a very close account of the room. Again there was no sign that Justice detected Demi anywhere within the very large area.

Finished scouting around the second safe room, Justice returned to Carson's side.

He looked up at his partner's face, waiting for further instructions, or the command that allowed him to lie down on the door and rest.

"Are these the only two safe rooms?" Carson asked her.

She laughed drily. "My father believes in overkill, but even he has his limits, so yes, these are the only two safe rooms in the mansion." She looked at Carson pointedly, expecting him to finally take his leave and go away. "Are you satisfied now?"

"Not by a long shot."

Chapter 11

Serena stared at the detective. He'd asked to see the safe rooms and she'd shown him the safe rooms—why wasn't the man leaving?

"What is that supposed to mean?" she wanted to know.

"It means," Carson said patiently, "I'm still looking for Demi."

"Even your dog doesn't think she's here," Serena pointed out. She petted Justice's head despite the canine's partner annoying the hell out of her. "You're welcome to continue turning over rocks on the property and looking for Demi, but I guarantee that no matter how long you spend here, you're going to have the same results," she told him, straightening up. "You're beating a dead horse, Detective. And where I'm from, that's offensive in too many ways to count."

"It's not my intention to offend you," Carson said as they left that wing.

"Good." She gave it another shot, hoping that this time she could induce him to leave. "Then go back to the police station or home or wherever it is you go after you clock out."

"Funny thing about police work," he told Serena. "You really don't get to 'clock out.' It's a twenty-four-hour-a-day, seven-days-a-week calling." His eyes met hers. "I can't go 'home.'"

She made her way to her wing of the mansion. "Sure you can. All you have to do is just get in that car of yours and drive away."

Maybe she forgot the exchange he'd had with her father when Judson had tried to get Serena to go with her family to the hotel. "I told your father that I'd look after you and your daughter."

Did he actually believe that was a compelling argument? "I'm sure he didn't take it to heart. You're a Gage. Not believing a word you say comes naturally to him."

"And living up to my word comes naturally to me," he countered. Maybe the idea of having him stay here made her uncomfortable. He could understand that. He didn't want to make her uncomfortable. "Don't worry, Justice and I will just sack out in one of the empty rooms upstairs. We won't get in your way."

Her eyes met his pointedly. He had got in her way from the first minute he'd stormed into the house that night, waving a warrant.

"Too late," she said.

Blowing out a breath, she tried to tell herself that he wasn't trying to annoy her. That he was just doing his job as a member of the police department. But if he had to be here, she didn't want him underfoot.

"There's food in the refrigerator in the kitchen. Why don't you go help yourself? I've got work in the stable," she said. Maybe keeping him informed of her work schedule would buy her a little good grace and some leeway.

When Carson followed her down the stairs with Justice, she didn't think anything of it. But when the two continued walking behind her as she headed for the front door, Serena stopped dead.

Pointing behind him, she said, "The kitchen's in the other direction."

"I know where the kitchen is," he answered matter-of-factly.

"So why aren't you headed there?" she wanted to know. "It might sound unusual to you, but that's where we keep the refrigerator."

"I'm not interested in the refrigerator," he told her in a no-nonsense voice. "I'm interested in keeping you alive."

Serena rolled her eyes. "Now you're just being melodramatic," she insisted.

And she was in denial, he thought. "You felt that bullet whiz by just like I did. That's not being melodramatic. That's just using the common sense that the good Lord gave each of us. Now, do yourself a favor and stop arguing with me."

"I don't need you hovering over me. I'll be fine," Serena insisted, pushing past him.

Not about to be shrugged off, Carson followed her outside.

Serena took exactly five steps then swung around to face him. How did she get through to this man? "Look, Detective, you're beginning to really annoy me."

"I'm not trying to do that, Ms. Colton," he said, reverting back to addressing her formally. "But someone killed my brother and now someone's taken a shot at you." His voice became deadly serious. "I don't intend to have you added to the body count on my watch."

Serena gave up. Trying to reason with the man was just a frustrating waste of time and she had things she wanted to do before nightfall, which came early this time of year. Besides, she thought, there was a small chance that he was right. She could take care of herself, but there was Lora's safety to think of. Better safe than sorry, she decided.

"Suit yourself," Serena told him as she continued on her way to the stables.

"I intend to," Carson murmured under his breath. Sparing a quick glance at Justice as they followed in Serena's wake, Carson said, "She's a regular spitfire, isn't she, boy?"

The dog made no sound, but Carson still took it as tacit agreement on the canine's part.

Carson had learned how to take in his surroundings and be vigilant without calling any attention to himself or what he was doing—and without missing a thing.

As daylight began to wane, he took note of Anders watching him in the distance, saw the handful of ranch hands the Double C foreman had working with him to reinforce a length of fence just beyond the corral. And all the while, he continued to look for something out of the ordinary, for that one thing that didn't mesh with everything else.

"Don't your eyes get tired, staring like that?" Serena finally asked him after she'd taken in the horse she'd been working with and brought out another from the stable.

Carson slid his gaze down the length of her, taking in every curve, every soft nuance her body had to offer. "Depends," he answered.

The man was as communicative as a rock, Serena thought, waiting for him to say something more.

When Carson didn't, she finally asked impatiently, "Depends on *what*?"

There was just possibly the smallest hint of a smile on his lips when he answered, "On what I'm staring at."

Serena knew he meant her but there was no way she could say anything about that without sounding full of herself or, at the very least, without borrowing trouble. All she could do was say something as enigmatic as what he'd just said.

"Careful your eyes don't get tread worn."

She saw the corners of his mouth curve just a tiny bit more as he answered, "I'll do my best."

Serena continued to feel like she was under a microscope, even when she looked up to see that Carson was scanning the horizon and not looking at her. Somehow, she thought, he was managing to do both.

Serena did her best to concentrate on the stallion she was working with and not on the man who had somehow done the impossible—he made her feel warm despite the cold temperature.

An hour later, exhausted, Serena decided to wrap it up and call it a day. The sun had gone down and it was really cold now. It was time to go in. Anders and his men had already gone to their quarters.

Bringing the stallion back into the stable, she brushed the horse down, the way she had the others and then walked out. Before she headed toward the mansion, she made sure to lock up the stable. In her present state of mind, the last thing she needed was for something to spook the horses and cause them to get out of the stable. She had no desire to spend hours tracking them down and rounding them up.

"You do this all the time?" Carson asked, picking up his pace as he and Justice fell into step beside her.

For just a moment, she'd forgotten he was there. It took all she had not to react as if the sound of his deep voice had startled her.

"Yes, when I'm not taking care of my daughter or going to horse auctions," she answered.

"You look like you're really good at it," Carson observed.

The detective was actually complimenting her, she realized. Serena hadn't expected that.

"I am," she answered. She wasn't boasting, she was just stating what she knew to be true.

"Must be nice to do something you're good at," Carson commented.

"It is." She'd enjoyed working with horses for as far back as she could remember. His comment piqued her curiosity about the man, who refused to go away. "How about you? Do you like what you do?"

His answer was vague, leaving it up to her to interpret. "I like keeping order," Carson replied.

Was that his way of avoiding telling her the truth? She decided to prod him a little. "I thought you like ordering people around."

Carson actually seemed to consider her question for a moment before giving her an answer. "That's part of it sometimes."

They'd reached the house and she, for one, was grateful. The walk from the stables to the mansion wasn't technically long enough to warm her. However it turned out to be long enough to make her aware of just how warm talking to him actually made her.

Opening the front door, the first thing that hit Serena was how quiet it all was. Her parents and sister made more noise than she'd realized. Shaking herself free of that thought, Serena proceeded to shrug out of her sheepskin jacket.

Hanging the jacket up in the hall closet, she turned toward Carson and asked, "Are you hungry now?"

Hunger had never governed his eating habits. He'd learned how to deal with perilous conditions and how to ignore a rumbling stomach. Ignoring it became a habit.

"I don't get hungry," he told her. "I eat to keep going."

"You sound like you have a lot in common with my horses," she commented. Feedings were carried out at regimented intervals.

The term "magnificent animal" suddenly flashed across her mind out of nowhere, catching her completely off guard and stunning her. The moment she thought of it, Serena realized that it just seemed to fit.

She found herself staring at Carson almost against her will.

"If you're trying to insult me, you haven't," he told her.

"I'm not insulting you," she said crisply. "But maybe I shouldn't have compared you to a horse. I find horses to be very noble animals."

He surprised her by laughing, but it wasn't at her. Her comment just seemed to tickle him.

"They are," he agreed. "And if you're interested, I don't fancy myself as being noble, just hardworking." He paused for a long moment, just looking at her. "Sometimes I just have to work harder than other times."

She struggled not to shiver. There was just something about the way he looked at her that caused her self-confidence to disintegrate into little tiny flakes that blew away in the wind.

"Why don't you go into the kitchen and have Sally whip up something for you?" she told him, referring to the cook. "I'm just going to go upstairs for a minute and check on Lora."

Carson never hesitated. He just started to walk upstairs with her. "I'll go with you."

Serena sighed. "You really are determined to be my shadow, aren't you?"

The detective said neither yes nor no. Instead, he told her, "Just doing whatever it takes to make sure that you and your daughter are safe."

Serena surrendered. She didn't even bother trying to argue with that.

* * *

The housekeeper was on her feet the moment Serena walked into her suite. The woman placed her finger to her lips, warning them not to raise their voices.

Crossing over to Serena, the housekeeper told her, "She just now fell asleep."

Serena lowered her voice to a whisper. "Did she give you any trouble?"

Alma shook her head, beaming. "No, she was a little darling. But she doesn't really sleep all that much for a three-month-old," she observed. "I was trying to keep her up so she'd sleep through the night for you, but just when I didn't want her to, she dozed off."

"Don't worry about it, Alma. I'm not planning on getting much sleep tonight anyway," Serena told the housekeeper.

Alma's eyes darted toward the man standing behind Serena. Understanding suddenly blossomed on the woman's round face. "Oh."

At that instant, it suddenly dawned on Serena what the housekeeper had to be thinking. She was about to protest and set the woman straight. But then she caught herself. She knew that if she protested, that would only convince the housekeeper that she was right in thinking there was something going on between her and the detective.

So, hard as it was, Serena pressed her lips together and kept silent about the misunderstanding.

Instead, she told the housekeeper, "I'm going to go downstairs and get some dinner. After I finish, I'll be back for the night. You'll be free to go on with your evening after that."

Stealing another long look at the detective, Alma said, "Take your time, Miss Serena. I don't mind staying here with your daughter. She's a little angel. Reminds me of my own when they were little."

As she and the detective walked out of the suite, Serena was positive the housekeeper was watching every step they took. The woman, she knew, was a great fan of romances, both on the screen and within the pages of a book. She had no doubt that Alma was probably fabricating a story about her and the brooding detective at this very moment.

The less said, the better, Serena decided.

Sally, the cook who was currently in her parents' employ—they had gone through an even dozen in as many years—was just cleaning up the kitchen when she and Carson walked in.

Immediately coming to attention when she saw them, Sally, a pleasant-faced woman in her early fifties, asked her, "What can I prepare for you and your guest, Miss Serena?"

"He's not my guest. He's a police detective, part of the K-9 division," Serena added before Sally could ask about the dog. She didn't want the cook to think that she was willingly entertaining Carson.

"What can I prepare for you and the police detective?" Sally asked, amending her initial question.

But Serena shook her head. "That's all right, Sally. You can take the rest of the evening off. I'll make something for myself. For us," she corrected, remembering to include the silent shadow beside her. Given what he'd said earlier, Carson probably ate nails or something of that nature.

Sally looked at her hesitantly. "Are you sure, Miss Serena?"

"My parents and sister have gone to stay in a hotel in town," she said by way of an answer, indicating that this was going to be an informal meal. "I'm sure."

"There are some leftovers on the two top shelves," the woman began, still not leaving.

"I'm good at scrounging, Sally. Go. You deserve some time off," Serena said, smiling as she waved the woman out.

Sally's smile was as wide as her face. "Thank you, miss!" she cried before she hurried off.

Turning back to the refrigerator, Serena found that the detective was already there.

"Can I help you find anything?" she asked him a little stiffly. It was a large kitchen, but somehow, it felt smaller to her because of his presence.

"No," Carson answered simply. Then, because she continued to stand there next to the refrigerator, he told her, "I'm good at scrounging, too."

Giving him space, Serena looked down at Justice. The dog was never more than a few paces away from his partner. "I don't have any dog food."

Carson didn't seem fazed. "That's okay. He adjusts. Same as me."

She wasn't sure exactly what that comment meant when it came to Carson, but she had an uneasy feeling that maybe this was the detective's way of putting her on some sort of notice.

As if she wasn't tense enough already.

Chapter 12

After watching Carson stand there, looking into the refrigerator without taking anything out, it was obvious to Serena that the detective either couldn't make up his mind, or he really didn't feel right about helping himself to something from the giant, industrial-size refrigerator.

Serena decided to take matters into her own hands. "Sit down, Gage," she said, elbowing Carson out of the way.

"Excuse me?" Carson made no move to do what she'd just very crisply ordered him to do, at least not until he knew what she was up to.

Okay, maybe she'd been a little too abrupt, Serena silently conceded. She decided to word her request a little better. "Well, you've taken it upon yourself to be my and my daughter's bodyguard so the least I can do is get you something to eat."

He didn't want her to feel she needed to wait on him. "I'm perfectly capable of getting something to eat for myself."

Serena rolled her eyes as she suppressed a sigh. "Does *everything* have to be an argument with you?" she asked. "Just sit!" she ordered.

Justice dropped down where he was standing, his big brown eyes trained on Serena. She laughed. "At least one of you doesn't have trouble following instructions."

"Hey," Carson pretended to protest. The protest was directed toward the German shepherd. "You're only supposed to listen to me, remember?" he told the canine.

"Too bad your dog can't teach you a few tricks," Serena quipped. Because the refrigerator was rather full and she had no idea what Carson would prefer eating, she asked, "Do you want a sandwich or a full meal?"

Carson had always leaned toward expediency. "A sandwich'll do fine."

There were sandwiches, and then there were *sandwiches*. "Okay, what do you want in your sandwich?"

Wide, muscular shoulders rose and fell in a dismissive, disinterested shrug. "Whatever you've got that's handy. I'm easy."

"Ha! Not hardly," Serena observed. His eyes met hers as if to contest her statement. However, Serena was not about to back down. "You, Detective Carson Gage, might be many things, but easy isn't one of them."

"And just what are some of those 'many things'?" Carson wanted to know, his eyes pinning her in place. He was ready for another argument.

There it was again, Serena thought. That flash of heat when he looked at her a certain way.

Stubbornly, Serena shut out her reaction, telling herself that she was smarter than that. There was no reason in the world for her to react like that to this rough-around-the-edges man or regard him as anything beyond a necessary evil.

Finished putting slices of freshly baked hickory-smoked ham on the extra thick bread that Sally baked for the family every other morning, she topped the sandwich off with slices of baby Swiss cheese. Serena put the whole thing on a plate with some lettuce and tomato slices on the side and pushed the plate over to him on the table.

"I see you finally sat down," she commented as she took out a bottle of ketchup and jars of mayonnaise and mustard. Serena paused over the last item. "Spicy or mild?"

Carson's mouth curved as he looked at her. "I like spicy."

There was that flash again, Serena thought in exasperation. She was just going to have to stop making eye contact with the man. But if she did that, he'd probably think she was avoiding him for some reason that she'd wind up finding insulting when he voiced it.

She took the jar of spicy mustard out of the refrigerator and placed it next to the other condiments. "Spicy, it is."

Eyes as dark as storm clouds on the horizon took measure of her as he reached for the mustard. He nodded toward the mayonnaise and the ketchup. "I don't need the others," he told her.

There was absolutely no reason for her heart to have sped up, Serena told herself. For pity's sake, it was just a conversation about some stupid mustard, nothing else. But she could feel her neck growing warmer, her palms getting damp and her knees felt as if they were getting ready to dissolve any minute now.

It was just the tension of recent events that were getting to her, Serena silently argued. A panic attack after the fact. Once everything got back to normal, so would she.

Carson took a bite of the large sandwich that now also included lettuce as well as a healthy slice of tomato.

"The ham's good," he pronounced.

Serena smiled. "I'll tell Sally you said so. She doesn't get any positive feedback from my family.

My mother usually berates her over things that she found lacking, things that poor Sally usually has no control over. Mother demands perfection—as well as mind reading—which would explain why we've been through a dozen cooks in the last twelve years," Serena commented, placing several slices of ham on a plate and then putting the plate in front of Justice.

The plate was cleaned before Carson had finished half his sandwich.

Done, Justice looked up at her, clearly waiting for more. When she made no attempt to move toward the refrigerator to give him more ham, Justice nudged her with his nose as if he was trying to get her to go back to "the magic box" that contained the meat.

"Justice, sit," Carson ordered sternly.

The canine instantly obeyed, looking rather dejected about it in Serena's opinion. Feeling sorry for the canine, Serena pulled a slice of ham out of the sandwich she had just fixed for herself.

She was about to give it to Justice when she heard Carson gruffly tell her, "Don't."

Startled, she looked in Carson's direction. Her eyes narrowed. "Are you ordering me around?"

Rather than answer her question, Carson felt it would be wiser to explain why he'd stopped her.

"Like the rest of the K-9s, Justice was painstakingly trained. If I give him a command and you do something that negates what I'm trying to convey to him, he's getting mixed signals that are bound to confuse him. There are times when my life depends on his reaction, and I'd rather that Justice wasn't confused."

Serena frowned. "I really doubt that he's going to have to defend you from being assaulted by a slice of ham," she told him sarcastically.

"The point I'm trying to get across is that disobedience just breeds more of the same," Carson informed her matter-of-factly. "And as I said, all the dogs that are part of the K-9 unit were very specifically trained."

"I know," she said, trying not to sound impatient, "by your brother."

But Carson shook his head. "Bo just raised the dogs," he told her. "He did some early work with them, but then the K-9 Training Center selected professional dog trainers for their program. Professional trainers like Hayley," he said, thinking of the woman Bo had been engaged to, "who worked with the dogs to train them for a number of diverse fields within the K-9 department. My brother definitely wasn't disciplined enough in his private life to train a goldfish, much less a German shepherd.

"Hell, Bo couldn't even discipline himself. Part of me," he admitted seriously, "is rather surprised that a jealous boyfriend didn't take him out long ago. Bo was always playing fast and loose, seeing one girl behind another one's back, jumping out of bedroom windows to avoid being on the wrong end of a jealous boyfriend's or enraged husband's gun."

Serena suddenly felt her opinion validated. "So you do have other people to investigate instead of just Demi," she cried.

"Yes and no," Carson said. "Bo actually settled down once he took up with Hayley," Carson said. Of course, he added silently, that had been for only the last three months, but it was a new pattern. "He didn't cheat on her, so jealous husbands and boyfriends were no longer prominently in the picture." He couldn't help thinking of what a terrible waste it all was. "I thought that maybe he finally grew up."

"Grew up?" Serena repeated, surprised. She thought about how Lora's father disappeared on her, taking her money and her credit cards with him. She'd been abandoned, humiliated *and* robbed, a veritable trifecta. "I thought that most men felt that this was the kind of lifestyle they aspired to—juggling women, enjoying them, then disappearing once it got too serious."

"I wouldn't know," Carson told her. "I never took a survey."

She decided the detective wasn't going to squirm out of giving her a straight answer. "How about you?" she pressed. "Did you look up to Bo? Did you want to be like him?"

Carson looked at her as if she had lost her mind. "Why the hell would I want to be like Bo? I'm already looking over my shoulder to make sure that there aren't any bad guys trying to take me out as it is. I wouldn't want to add disgruntled husbands and angry ex-girlfriends to that number."

He almost sounded as if he meant it. Serena caught herself wanting to believe him, but her experience with Lora's father had tainted her.

"So then you're monogamous?" she asked.

"What I am," Carson told her with a finality that said he wanted to be done with this conversation, "is focused on my job. That takes up all of my time. Right, Justice?" he asked, looking at the dog.

Justice barked, then looked at Serena. The German shepherd began to drool, clearly eyeing the remainder of her sandwich.

Serena, in turn, looked at Carson. "Here," she said, pushing her plate and what was left of her sandwich toward him. "You give it to Justice. I wouldn't want to interfere with the connection you two have."

"Justice," Carson said sternly. The dog immediately became alert, looking at Carson and waiting for his next command. "At ease."

With that, the canine relaxed, almost flopping down on the floor.

"Okay, now you can give that to him," he told Serena, nodding at what was left of her sandwich.

She could only stare at him, stunned. "'At ease'? You're kidding."

"No," he answered. "Training is training. Trust

me, this is for everyone's own good. Justice has to know who to listen to. If I tell him 'at ease,' he knows it's okay with me if he goes with his instincts."

"All that with 'at ease'?" she said, marveled but somewhat skeptical nonetheless.

"There's a little more to it than that," Carson admitted. Now, however, wasn't the time to get into it. It was getting late. "But yeah."

She shook her head, then held out her sandwich to Justice. The dog quickly consumed every last bite, carefully eating it out of her hand.

His teeth never once even came close to nipping her skin.

When the sandwich was gone, Serena brushed off her hands against one another, still marveling at how gentle Justice had been.

"You're right," she told Carson. "Your dog is very well trained."

"He's not my dog," Carson corrected her. "He's my partner. Best partner I ever had," he said, affectionately petting the animal and ruffling Justice's black-and-tan fur. "He doesn't mouth off, doesn't give me any grief and always has my back."

"Sounds like a match made in heaven," Serena commented.

"It pretty much is," Carson agreed.

He got up and carried his empty plate to the sink. She expected the detective to leave his plate there and was surprised to see him wash the plate and place it in the rack to dry.

Turning around to see that she was watching him, Carson made an assumption as to what she was probably thinking.

"I wasn't raised in a barn," he told her.

"I didn't think you were," she assured him quickly. "It's just that nobody does that around here," she explained. "I mean, I do sometimes, but Anders doesn't take his meals here and my parents and sister just assume that's what the housekeeper is for. In their opinion, it's all just part of 'keeping the house.'"

She'd managed to arouse his curiosity again. "What makes you so different from them?" he asked.

She hadn't given it much thought. It was just something that had always been that way. Since he asked, Serena thought for a moment before answering.

"I think for myself. And I like working with the horses." She thought of the way Joanelle turned her nose up at things. "My mother wouldn't be caught dead near the corral unless the rest of the ranch was on fire. Maybe not even then," she amended with a whimsical smile.

Serena realized that the detective had grown quiet and was just studying her. She'd said too much, she admonished herself.

Clearing her throat, she picked up her own plate

and glass and made her way over to the sink, where she washed them.

"I'd better be getting back up to Lora," she told him, paving the way for her retreat. "She's probably waking up about now. Poor Alma's practically put in a full day taking care of her. It might not look it, but taking care of a baby is exhausting. Alma doesn't complain, but I know she'd welcome having the rest of the evening to herself. With the rest of the family gone, there won't be any sudden 'emergencies' cropping up."

When Carson began to follow her out of the kitchen, she was quick to try to divert him.

"You don't have to come up right away. There's a big-screen TV in the entertainment room if you want to watch anything." She gestured toward the large room as she passed it on her way to the staircase.

"I'm not here to watch TV," he told her. "I'm here to watch you."

"I didn't think you meant that literally," she protested. At the very most, she'd thought he'd just be somewhere on the premises, not really with her. Not for the night.

Carson could almost read her mind. "I don't intend to hover over you, if that's what you're afraid of, Serena. But I do intend to be close by."

Serena made her way up the stairs, then paused and turned around. She was two steps above Carson. Just enough to bring them eye to eye, literally rather than figuratively.

"Define 'close by.'"

"A room near your suite," he answered. "Or I can just bed down in front of your door if need be."

What she needed, Serena thought, attempting to reconcile herself to this turn of events, was to get her life back.

She blew out a breath. "You really intend to go through with this."

"I said I would and I always live up to my word."

"Why couldn't you be a liar like every other man?" she murmured under her breath as she turned around and started to go up the stairs again.

He couldn't make out what she'd said, only that Serena had said something. "What?"

Serena merely sighed and continued walking up the stairs. There was no point in repeating what she'd said. "Never mind."

Chapter 13

The housekeeper was on her feet the moment that Serena walked into the suite.

Serena could see by the look on Alma's face that the woman seemed very interested in the fact that Carson still hadn't left the Double C.

Not only hadn't the detective left it, but he gave no indication that he was going anywhere this evening.

Normally, Serena prided herself as being a private person who didn't go out of her way to justify her actions. What people thought about her was their own business and she was not in the habit of making any excuses. But she liked Alma. The woman had been exceptionally helpful and kind to her, especially when she'd been pregnant with Lora.

Right now, she could see that Alma was dying to ask questions, but her mother had been very specific when it came to what her "place" was as a housekeeper for Judson Colton and his family. Consequently, the woman would explode before asking anything concerning why the detective was still here.

"Justice and I are going to take a look around the second floor," the detective told Serena, walking out of her room. "We're going to make sure that there's nobody up here, present company excepted."

Serena waited until Carson was out of earshot. "Alma," she began. "I'm going to need you to bring some bedding into the spare bedroom that's next to my suite. Detective Gage is spending the night," she added, watching the housekeeper.

Alma's expression remained impassive. She nodded dutifully. "Very good, Miss Serena."

"No, it isn't," Serena corrected, knowing exactly what was going through the other woman's head. "But it is what it is and we're just going to have to deal with it for the night." That didn't come out right, Serena thought. She tried again. "It's the detective's intention to stand guard over us to make sure that Lora and I stay safe."

This time she saw Alma smile, sanctioning what the detective was doing. "Very good, Miss Serena."

"Then you approve?" Serena asked, trying to find out just what the woman thought of the whole setup. As for herself, she hadn't reconciled herself to the idea of having Carson hovering around like a brooding guardian angel.

"It's not my place to approve or disapprove, Miss Serena. I'm only supposed to follow orders," Alma replied quietly.

"But you must have an opinion," Serena pressed.

"I am not being paid to have an opinion, Miss Serena. Only to make things as comfortable as possible for you and your family." When Serena gave her a look that clearly said she wanted the woman to give voice to something a little more personal than that, Alma gave every indication that her lips were sealed.

And then the housekeeper leaned in a little closer to the young woman, who, unlike her parents and younger sister, always treated her with kindness and respect.

Lowering her voice, Alma said, "It's a good thing to have someone so capable and good-looking watching over you."

Serena bit back a laugh despite herself. Obviously Carson's looks had won the housekeeper over. "I didn't know you noticed things like that, Alma."

"I'm not dead, miss," the woman replied just as Carson and his four-footed partner returned to the suite.

Carson looked from the housekeeper to Serena. Judging from the housekeeper's expression and the sudden onset of silence as he walked in, he guessed that something was up. "Did I miss something?" he asked after the other woman left the room.

Serena looked at him with wide-eyed innocence. "I thought you never missed anything," she told him. "Isn't that why you're here?"

She was clearly baiting him. He deliberately ignored it. Instead, he merely gave her his report. "Justice and I swept through your floor. Everything looks to be in order."

She couldn't explain why, but Carson's solemn expression just made her want to laugh. "Nobody's hiding in the closet?"

His eyes went flat. "This isn't a joke, Serena," he said gruffly. "Someone took a shot at you today."

She was not about to allow herself to be paralyzed by fear. "I'm really not worried about someone who can't hit the broadside of a barn," Serena told him.

He didn't like the fact that she was taking all this so lightly. Didn't she realize the very real danger she could be in?

"Maybe they can and they're just toying with you first," Carson pointed out. "Are you willing to bet your daughter's life that you're right?" he demanded, struggling to keep his voice down so as not to wake up the sleeping baby.

Serena frowned, glancing over her shoulder toward the crib. "You really do know how to get to a person, don't you?"

Carson definitely didn't see it that way. "If I did," he

told Serena, "you and your daughter would be in town by now, staying in the hotel with the rest of your family."

This wasn't going anywhere, and she was not about to just stand here, listening to him go over what he viewed as her shortcomings.

"My housekeeper put fresh linens in the guest room for you," she told the detective. "It's this way." Crossing to the doorway of her bedroom, she found Carson blocking her exit. She could see that he wasn't about to go anywhere. She glared at the man. "I can't walk through you," she said pointedly.

He had no desire to be down the hall from her. If something went wrong, seconds would count. "That's okay. Justice and I'll just bunk down outside your door. It's closer that way," he emphasized.

Enough was enough. "Aren't you carrying this whole thing a little too far?" she asked, irritated. "If this person is dumb enough to show up here, we're dealing with someone with an ax to grind, not a professional cat burglar who's light on their feet."

And then Serena decided to attempt to use another tactic.

"Alma made the bed up for you," she reminded him. "If you don't use it, the woman's feelings will be hurt and heaven knows my family's done enough of a number on her. To be honest, I have no idea why Alma puts up with it and stays."

Carson laughed shortly and shook his head at her

in wonder. "And that's supposed to get me to use the guest room?"

"No," she corrected, "common sense is supposed to do that. Besides, you're probably the type who sleeps with one eye and both ears open, so if anyone does try to break in and shoot me, you'll hear them before they get off a shot."

Carson knew she was mocking him. But he also knew that he wasn't about to get anywhere arguing with her. Justice was with him; he was confident that the German shepherd would alert him if anyone who didn't belong on the premises entered the house.

So, because it was getting late, and in the interest of peace, Carson gave in. "Okay, you win. If you need me, I'll be in the guest room."

Serena looked at him in surprise. She'd expected him to put up more of a fight than this. Was he up to something?

"You're being reasonable?" she asked, looking at him uncertainly.

The expression on her face was worth the capitulation. "It's been known to happen."

She decided it was best to call it a night before Carson decided to change his mind and resurrect the argument.

"Good, then if you don't mind, I'm going to try to get some sleep while my daughter's still napping." She gestured to the open door down the hall. "That's your room. I'll see you in the morning, Detective."

"Yes," he assured her, standing there a moment longer and looking at her, "you will."

Why did such a simple sentence cause her to suddenly feel hot ripples going up and down her skin? He wasn't saying anything out of the ordinary. The detective was agreeing with her, for pity's sake.

So why did she feel as if he'd just set up some sort of a secret rendezvous between them?

He hadn't done anything of the sort, Serena silently insisted, firmly closing her bedroom door behind her. All he'd said was that he'd see her in the morning, which right now seemed like an inevitable fact of life. But by no means was he making some sort of an earthshaking revelation.

Was he?

She was getting punchy, Serena told herself with a sigh. Punchy. That was why she wasn't thinking straight and coming up with all these strange thoughts and reactions.

She supposed that, in all honesty, the missed shot really had unnerved her.

What if it *had* been someone out to shoot her?

But why? Why would anyone want to shoot *her*? She just didn't understand. No one had come out and threatened her and she certainly wasn't a threat to anyone. It all had to be some kind of a gross misunderstanding, and the sooner it was cleared up, the sooner she would be able to get back to her old life.

Her relatively uneventful, humdrum life, she

thought as she sat pulling a hairbrush through her hair, something she had done religiously ever since she'd been old enough to hold her own hairbrush.

Feeling exceptionally tired all of a sudden, Serena gave up brushing her hair and laid the brush aside.

She slipped into the nursery, checking on her daughter. The crib had just been moved there from her own room yesterday. Lingering, she watched Lora sleep for a minute or two, then crossed back to her bedroom. Mechanically turning off the lamp, Serena crawled into bed, bone weary beyond words.

She was asleep within less than five minutes.

It was the dream that woke her. A dream that a tall slender person had slipped into her room and was now running off with her daughter.

A scream rose in her throat, but try as she might, Serena just couldn't make herself release it, couldn't scream to alert Carson so that he could come and rescue her daughter.

Oh, why hadn't she allowed him to spend the night on the floor right outside her suite the way he'd wanted to? The kidnapper would have never got in to steal her baby if Carson had been standing guard right by her door.

Frightened, she tried to scream again, but nothing came out. It was as if her throat had been sealed shut.

Just like her eyes. They were shut, too, she realized. Shut and practically glued together.

Was that it? Were they glued shut?

Why couldn't she open her eyes? She needed to be able to see the person who had broken into her suite. The person who had just made off with her baby.

How could she give Carson a description of the fiend when she couldn't see him?

A hot wave of desperation washed over Serena as she tried to scream again. To make some kind of a noise, any kind of a noise, in order to scare away the intruder.

No sounds came.

She felt absolutely powerless.

Carson wasn't in the habit of falling asleep while on duty. It had never happened to him before. He prided himself on being able to get by with next to no sleep for several days on end.

But he'd been going nonstop for more than a few days now and though he really hated to admit it, hated what it ultimately said about his stamina, it had finally caught up to him.

Carson didn't remember his eyes shutting. But they must have because the next thing he knew, they were flying open, pried open by a sound.

A sound that had seeped into his consciousness.

The sound of Justice's nails along the marble floor as he suddenly scrambled up, completely alert.

Carson was still groggy and half-asleep, but he knew that his K-9 partner had been awakened by something.

Or someone.

Suddenly as alert as his dog, Carson immediately scanned the darkened room, searching for movement, for some minute indication that something was out of place.

Everything was just the way it had been when he'd settled back on the bed.

But he knew he'd heard something.

And from the way Justice had gained his feet, so had the German shepherd.

Opening the door ever so carefully, Carson slipped out into the hall. Nothing was moving, nothing was out of place.

Maybe he'd been dreaming after all.

But glancing at Justice told him that it wasn't a dream. Something was definitely up.

Exercising the same stealth movements, Carson opened the door leading into Serena's suite. He knew he ran the risk of having her think he was taking advantage of the situation, but that really didn't matter in this case. His gut was telling him to push on.

Something was up.

Moving in almost painfully slow motion, Carson opened Serena's door. With his fingertips against the highly polished door, he eased it back until he was able to look into the room.

It was cold, unusually cold.

The door between the bedroom and the nursery was open.

A movement in the nursery caught his eye.

As his vision acclimated to the darkness, Carson saw a tall slender figure dressed completely in black leaning over the baby's crib.

Reaching in.

Carson had his gun in his hand, but he couldn't risk taking a shot. The dark figure was too close to Lora.

"Freeze!" he ordered in a loud, menacing voice.

Startled, the figure bolted toward the open balcony doors on the other side of Serena's bedroom.

Serena had jackknifed upright in bed and screamed when she realized that someone was in her room. Instinctively, she knew that her daughter's life was in danger.

She hadn't been dreaming; this was very real!

Justice and then Carson whizzed by her bed, running toward the balcony. There was a new moon out so there was nothing to illuminate her room and help her see what was happening.

She sensed rather than saw that someone was in her suite. It was possibly more than just one person.

Serena quickly turned on the lamp next to her bed. Light flooded the room at the same time that she reached into the nightstand drawer. She pulled out the handgun she always kept there.

Carson and Justice had reached the balcony, but they were too late to stop the fleeing potential kidnapper. All Carson saw was a dark figure who had managed to get down to the ground unhurt and was now sprinting away from the mansion.

The darkness quickly swallowed the would-be kidnapper up.

"Damn it," Carson cursed under his breath. His weapon was still drawn, but he wasn't about to shoot at what he couldn't really see.

Turning back toward the suite, he went in and was about to close the door—by now the suite was absolutely freezing—when he saw Serena. She was pointing a handgun at him.

"Whoa, whoa, whoa," he cautioned, raising one hand while the other still held his weapon. "Put that thing down. I'm one of the good guys, remember?"

But Serena kept her weapon trained on him. She wasn't about to lower it until he answered some questions to her satisfaction. She was breathing hard and her heart was racing like crazy.

It took her a second to catch her breath. "What just happened?" she wanted to know.

Turning his back on her, Carson secured the balcony doors and then turned around to face her. "As near as I can figure it, Justice and I just stopped someone from kidnapping your baby."

Serena's arms sagged. The handgun she was holding suddenly felt as if it weighed a ton.

With concentrated effort, she put it back in the open drawer. All she could do was stare at the detective, dumbfounded.

Her throat almost closed up as she cried, "Kidnapping?"

Chapter 14

"That's what I said," Carson confirmed quietly with just the slightest nod of his head as he looked at her. "Kidnapping."

If anything, the idea of someone shooting at her ultimately made Serena angry. She could deal with that, find a way to fight back and defend herself. It was in her nature to fight back.

But the thought of someone kidnapping her child, that was an entirely different matter. That was scary.

She could feel a cold chill not only running up and down her spine, but gripping her heart and squeezing it so hard that she could barely breathe.

She moved over to the crib in the nursery. Somehow, Lora had slept through all the commotion. Serena felt a very real desire to stand here forever and just watch her daughter sleep. The scene was such a contrast to what *could* have happened.

"Who would want to kidnap Lora?" Serena wanted to know, her voice quavering as she tried to come to terms with the frightening thought.

Carson shrugged. He moved a little closer to Serena but still managed to maintain a safe distance. He didn't want her to feel that he was crowding her. He just wanted her to realize that he was there for her. For her daughter and her.

"Maybe Demi was looking for some leverage to use to get the police off her back."

"Demi again," Serena cried, stunned. She moved away from the crib, taking their conversation to the threshold between her bedroom and the nursery. "You think that Demi Colton is behind this, too," she said incredulously, then demanded, "Are you kidding me?"

Carson's expression was deadly serious. "That shadowy figure could have easily matched a description of Demi's body type."

At another time, she might have been rendered speechless, but this was about her daughter as well and she needed Carson to find whoever was behind this threat—and it *wasn't* Demi.

"Good Lord, by the time you're done, Demi Colton is going to be behind every crime committed in the county, maybe even in this part of the state." Did he see how ludicrous what he'd just said sounded? "Demi's smart, I'll give you that. But she isn't some kind of criminal mastermind," Serena cried.

"What is this obsession you have with her?" she wanted to know. And then, as if hearing the exasperation in her own voice, Serena took a breath and backed off. "Look, I'm sorry. You saved my baby, and I am very grateful to you. I didn't mean to go off on you like that." She dragged her hand through her hair. "I guess I'm just on edge. But I think I got a better look at whoever was in my room than you did—"

Carson was immediately alert. "You saw the kidnapper's face?"

She only wished she had. "No, the kidnapper had on a ski mask. But whoever it was that ran by was too tall to be Demi."

Carson wasn't so sure. "Demi's about five foot nine, five foot ten and slim. The kidnapper was under six feet and on the thin side."

But Serena just shook her head. "No, it's not her," she said with conviction. "She doesn't need to steal *my* baby."

There was something in Serena's voice that he couldn't quite put his finger on. Maybe she was just being overly protective of the other woman.

Carson pressed on. "Maybe she wants to hold your daughter for ransom. She knows you'll pay whatever she asks and a big payoff will go a long way in setting her up in a new life somewhere else." And then he stopped, thinking. If the kidnapper had tried once, maybe Demi, or whoever it was, would try again. "Maybe you should reconsider staying at the hotel with your family until this blows over."

But that was definitely the wrong thing to say to her. "No. I'm not going to let whoever's doing this run me off my own land," Serena said fiercely.

There was bravery—and then there was such a thing as being *too* brave without considering the consequences. "Even if it means putting your daughter in danger?" Carson wanted to know.

"I have you to protect her, don't I?" Serena responded. She could feel anger bubbling up inside of her. "And just what kind of a mother would I be, teaching my daughter that it's all right to run at the first sign of trouble?"

Serena had leaped out of her bed when he and Justice had raced into the room. Confronted with the possibility of her daughter being stolen, she hadn't thought to put on a robe.

She still hadn't, and now he found himself wishing that she would. It wasn't his place to say anything. The nightgown she was wearing wasn't exactly transparent, but it did cause his imagination to wreak havoc.

Carson forced himself to focus on what had almost just happened and not on the tantalizing way her breasts rose and fell.

"Your daughter is three months old. I don't think she'll know the difference if you dig in or leave," he told her sternly.

Serena's eyes flashed. Did he think that she was going to hide behind the fact that her daughter was an infant? "Maybe she won't," she agreed. "But I'll know."

There were several choice words he wanted to say to her about taking risks and being foolhardy, words that were hovering on the tip of his tongue. With steely resolve, Carson managed to refrain from uttering any of them.

Instead, he merely grunted in response to the sentiment she'd expressed. He was learning that arguing with the woman was just an exercise in futility.

"Justice and I are going to have another look around the place, make sure your night caller didn't get it into his head to double back and try again." He crossed to the balcony, checking to make sure that the doors leading out were still locked. "When I leave, I want you to lock your doors. Don't open them to anyone."

"Except for you," she amended, certain he had omitted that part of the instruction.

"You don't have to concern yourself with me," he told her. He nodded toward her bed. "Just try to get some sleep before morning."

Right. Sleep. Easy for you to say, Serena thought

as she closed her bedroom doors behind Carson and then locked them.

She went to the balcony doors and checked them even though she had seen Carson lock them earlier and just check them before he left.

She crossed back into the nursery. It amazed her again that Lora had not only slept through the kidnapping threat but had slept through the raised voices, as well. As for her, she knew that there was no way she was going to get back to sleep, not in her present frame of mind. Every sound that she would hear—or *thought* she heard—was going to be magnified to twice its volume, if not more.

Resigned, Serena didn't even bother lying down. Instead, she decided just to sit and keep vigil in the oversize rocker-recliner that Anders had got her as a gift when Lora was born.

Wanting to be fully prepared for whatever might happen, Serena took her handgun out of the nightstand drawer and put it on the small table next to the rocker-recliner.

Sitting down, she proceeded to wait for the intruder to return or for dawn to break, whatever would happen first.

Serena was still in the recliner when daybreak finally came. It seemed like an eternity later to her and she felt somewhat stiff after spending what was left of the night in an upright sitting position.

But she'd had no intention of being caught off guard again if the intruder returned. An aching body was more than a fair trade-off to knowing her daughter was safe.

As it was, the only "intruder" she had to deal with was Lora, who woke up twice in the last few hours, once because she was wet, once because she was hungry. Taking care of both needs as they arose, Serena returned her daughter to her crib and each time Lora obligingly went back to sleep.

Feeling achy and stiff, Serena really wanted to take a shower, but she wanted to make sure that nothing else had gone down during the past night. She'd half expected Carson to check in on her. When he hadn't, she just assumed that he and his German shepherd had gone back to the guest room.

However the more time that passed, the more uneasy she became. So finally, pausing only to throw on some clothes, Serena opened her bedroom door, ready to go and knock on the guest room door in order to wake Carson up.

She didn't have to.

Carson was right there, sitting cross-legged on the floor in front of her door. The second she opened the door, the detective was up on his feet—and Justice was right there beside him.

Startled, she was quick to silence the gasp that rose to her lips. She did her best to look unfazed about finding him even though the exact opposite was true. Bending down to pet Justice—the canine appeared to have taken a liking to her—she was able to effectively mask her surprise.

"I thought you were going to spend the night in the guest room," she said, straightening up.

"Never said that," Carson reminded her. He was relieved that she'd got dressed before coming out, although there was a part of him that had to admit he'd liked the previous view.

"You spent the whole night on the floor outside my bedroom?" Serena questioned. Who did that when there was a comfortable bed only yards away?

"There wasn't a whole night left after the kidnapper ran off," he corrected.

Serena sighed. Her surprised observation wasn't meant to be the opening line for a debate.

"Isn't *anything* a simple yes or no with you?" she asked, frustrated that there wasn't such a thing as a simple conversation when it came to this man.

"No," he answered honestly.

The maddening impossibility of the whole situation suddenly hit her and Serena started to laugh.

Her laughter was infectious and after a minute, Carson's laughter blended with hers. The laughter continued for more than a couple of minutes and managed to purge some of the ongoing tension that was shimmering between them.

It also managed to draw the housekeeper, who was already up and dressed, to Serena's suite.

The woman made a quick assessment of her own about the state of affairs. Alma looked from Serena to the detective, then smiled. "Apparently, from the sound of it, the night went well."

Serena decided to wait to tell the woman about the aborted kidnapping after she had a chance to get some coffee into her system.

So all she said in response now was, "Well, we're still here."

Alma nodded, looking pleased. "Yes, so I see. There's a pot of fresh coffee downstairs," she told Serena.

"Music to my ears, Alma," Serena responded.

Obviously thinking that the two were about to go downstairs to the kitchen, the housekeeper offered, "If you give me a moment, I'll get Sally up to make you breakfast."

But Serena waved away the suggestion. "No, don't bother. Let Sally sleep in for once. I can handle breakfast for the detective and myself," Serena told the housekeeper.

"Are you sure, Miss Serena?" Alma asked.

"I'm sure," she told the housekeeper. "As long as you watch Lora for me."

"Consider it done," Alma answered with pleased enthusiasm.

"Should I be worried?" Carson asked Serena as they went downstairs.

Reaching the landing, Serena went on to the

kitchen. The house seemed almost eerily quiet to her. She was accustomed to hearing her mother's voice raised in displeasure, ordering someone around.

"Only if you get me angry when I have a frying pan in my hand," Serena replied. "But if you're referring to my cooking, I haven't poisoned anyone yet."

It was hard for him to believe that a pampered Colton was serious about making breakfast. "I didn't know you cooked."

"Lots of things about me you don't know," she answered. Opening one of the refrigerator doors, she took out four eggs. "I don't like being waited on," she went on, "so I learned how to cook."

Putting the eggs on the counter, she paused as she reached for some bread. And then it occurred to her that she had just assumed what he wanted for breakfast without asking.

Turning toward Carson now, she remedied the situation. "I didn't ask you. Eggs and toast okay, or do you want something else? I can make pancakes or waffles, or—"

"Eggs and toast will be fine," he answered before she could go through an entire litany of all the different things that came under the heading of breakfast.

"Eggs and toast, it is," Serena agreed. "How do you want your eggs?"

He'd already told her last night that he was generally indifferent to food. "Any way but raw."

Serena laughed in response.

He wasn't aware that he'd said anything amusing. "What's so funny?"

She shook her head. She supposed that the man just didn't see it. "Anyone who didn't know you would say you were easy."

So far, he still didn't see what was so amusing to Serena. "I *am* easy."

She put four slices into the toaster, adjusting the lever for medium.

"You keep telling yourself that, Carson."

"I *am* easy," Carson stressed. "I have few requirements." Serena handed him a cup of black coffee. He accepted it automatically. "One of which is that I don't like being lied to."

She stopped pouring coffee into her mug and turned to look at him. Was he deliberately being enigmatic, or was he just fishing for a response from her? "Are you saying I did?"

Carson raised one eyebrow, his gaze pinning hers. "Did you?"

Serena never flinched or looked away. Instead, she raised her chin defiantly and told him, "No."

Carson decided to believe her—unless she gave him reason not to. "Then we should keep it that way," he told her.

"No problem here." She took a long sip of her coffee, then turned her attention to preparing the rest of the breakfast. "By the way, does that go both ways?"

"Are you asking me if I lied to you?" Carson wanted to know.

Two could play at this vague game of his. "I am."

His voice was dead serious as he answered her. "I didn't."

Maybe she was just being naively foolish, but she believed him. Or maybe she just wanted to feel that there was someone on her side. "Looks like everything's just coming up roses between us then," she responded. And then she saw him grin. "What?"

"That strange, ungodly sound that you're hearing are dead Coltons and Gages, collectively rolling over in their graves," he said.

Buttering the slices of toast that had just popped up, she laughed. "They would, wouldn't they? You know, I kind of like that idea, doing something to cause past generations of Coltons and Gages to roll over in their graves.

"I always thought the idea of a family feud was the stupidest waste of time imaginable," she continued. "That sort of thing belongs to the Hatfields and the McCoys, not to people who live in the twenty-first century," Serena said as she scrambled the four eggs together in a large frying pan. Looking at the pan, she grinned. "My mother would be horrified if she saw me making a Gage breakfast in our kitchen. Hell, she'd be horrified if she saw me making breakfast, period, but especially for a Gage," she told him.

"I said you didn't have to," he reminded her.

Detective or not, the man could be very dense, Serena thought. "You're missing the point," she told him.

"I guess I am," he was willing to admit. "Educate me. What is the point?"

She lowered the temperature under the frying pan. "That two intelligent families feuding over something that happened between two people decades ago is stupid and anyone with half a brain should definitely not allow themselves to be pulled into this feud."

"Do I qualify as someone with half a brain?" he wanted to know, amused by her description.

Still scrambling the eggs, Serena looked at him. "At least half," she deadpanned.

"Thanks."

"Don't mention it," she managed to say before the grin won out, curving her mouth. "Get a couple of plates from the cupboard, will you?"

There was no shortage of cupboards and cabinets in the large kitchen. He could be opening and closing doors for several minutes.

"You want to point me in the right direction?" he asked.

Responding, Serena moved the frying pan off the active burner. "Typical male," she commented with amusement. Hands on his shoulders, she literally pointed Carson toward the cupboard that held the everyday dishes. "That one," she told him.

He knew it was his imagination, but he could swear that he felt the warmth from her hands coming through his shirt, seeping into his shoulders. The warmth found its way into his system, spreading out through all of him.

He hadn't been with a woman since Lisa had died, and for some reason, he was acutely aware of that lack right at this moment. Aware of the fact that it had been eating away at him, bit by bit, from the first time he had laid eyes on her.

"Are you all right?" Serena asked when he made no move toward the cupboard.

"Yeah." Carson forced himself to shake off the feeling that was taking hold of him and got the plates she'd requested. He placed them on the counter. "Just wondering why anyone would need this many cabinets, that's all."

"That's an easy one to answer," she told him, dividing the eggs between the two plates. The mansion belonged to her mother when her father had married her and Joanelle was responsible for every part of its decor. "For show."

Chapter 15

"For show?" Carson repeated as Serena took her seat at the table.

He thought he understood what she was saying, but he wanted to make sure he wasn't assuming too much, so he waited for a little clarification.

And Serena had no problem giving it. "It is my mother's life ambition to make every other living person be in total awe and envy of her—and she won't rest until that happens." As far as she was concerned, her mother's attitude was deplorable, but she wasn't about to say it out loud.

Joanelle Colton's shallowness was nothing new as far as Carson was concerned. He shrugged, paying far more attention to his bracing cup of coffee than to the conversation.

After taking a long sip, he quipped, "I guess everyone should have a goal in life."

"Well, the baby and I definitely put a crimp in her goal," she commented more to herself than to Carson as she quickly consumed her breakfast. She had a full day ahead of her and she needed to get to it.

Carson, however, seemed to have other ideas. Serena was about to get up when he asked her another question.

"Earlier, you said that Demi didn't need to kidnap your daughter. What did you mean by that?" The way she had phrased it—as well as her tone of voice—had been preying on his mind.

That had been a slip on her part, Serena thought. She shouldn't have said anything.

She shrugged now, trying to dismiss the whole thing. "Oh, you know. The usual."

"No," he answered, not about to let the matter go so easily. "I don't know. Enlighten me." As he looked at her across the table, Carson once again had the distinct feeling that there was something she wasn't telling him. "Serena, if you're holding something back, I need to know. What is it you're not telling me?" he pressed. "You used the word *need* before. Was that just you talking a mile a minute, trying to find a way to make me stop looking at Demi as a suspect, or was there something more to this? I know that she took a lot of cash with her, but that doesn't mean she has enough to fund being on the run."

When Serena made no answer, it just reinforced the idea that he was on to something. "*Why* did you say she didn't *need* to kidnap your baby? Oh wait— you mean because she's pregnant herself."

He was crowding her and Serena lost her temper. "Exactly. She's going to have one of her own," she snapped. "That's all I meant. The idea of her kidnapping Lora for ransom is ludicrous and never would have occurred to me."

Serena stared up at the kitchen's vaulted ceiling, searching for strength.

"As I already asked, please don't say anything to anyone," she implored, looking into his eyes, trying to make contact with his soul—if he had one. "Demi didn't want anyone else to know. She only told me because she thought that I'd understand since I'd just gone through the same thing myself."

Carson looked at her, debating whether or not he was buying this. He hadn't told Finn, despite the pregnancy speaking to motive, no matter what Serena had said in opposition about how Demi wouldn't kill her child's father. Maybe because he wasn't sure yet if Demi was really pregnant at all. For reasons of her own, Serena might have made up the pregnancy to get him to feel sorry for Demi or go easier on her cousin.

For the moment, he decided to go along with

Serena's story. "And she was sure that Bo was the father?"

Serena nodded. "Yes."

He waited, but Serena didn't say anything further. Instead, she reached over and gathered his empty plate, then stacked it on top of hers.

Carson put his hand over hers, stopping her from getting up with the plates.

"You said he didn't know about the baby."

"Right. Demi didn't want to tell him yet. He was marrying someone else. She didn't want to look as if she was trying to get him to call off the wedding and marry her instead. She didn't *want* him to marry her. Demi told me she had finally come to her senses and realized that Bo was loathsome—no offense."

"None taken." Serena wasn't giving voice to anything that hadn't crossed his mind about his brother more than once.

Serena went on to tell the detective, "Demi told me that she wouldn't marry Bo if he was dipped in gold and covered with diamonds."

He wondered if Demi had laid it on a little thick to cover her tracks. "Pretty harsh words for the father of her baby," Carson observed.

"Demi had caught him cheating on her more than once and, don't forget, they'd broken up," Serena reminded him. "Bo being the baby's father was just an unforeseen accident."

He saw the pregnancy in a slightly different light. "Certainly gives her motive to kill Bo."

He was back to that again? Serena rolled her eyes in exasperation. "Only if she'd wanted something from him, which she *didn't*. All Demi wanted before Bo went and got himself killed was just to have her baby and make a life for the two of them."

"Well, the simplest thing for Demi to do would be just to—"

Serena knew what he was going to say. He was going to say that Demi should do what her mother had told her to do when she had to tell her parents that she was pregnant. She cut Carson short before he was able to finish his sentence.

"No, that's not the 'simplest thing' for some women," she informed Carson, annoyed that he'd even think to suggest it. "For some women, that would be the worst course of action to take. Besides," she passionately maintained, "it's a baby, not a mistake."

Taking a breath, she forced herself to calm down. "But all that aside, you can see why she wouldn't want to kidnap my baby. She's already got one on the way to worry about."

"Yes, but a sizable ransom would go a long way to helping her raise that baby," Carson reminded her again.

"Except for one thing," Serena countered.

"What's that?"

"I already offered to *give* Demi money to see her through this, and she turned me down," she told the detective. "She wouldn't just turn around and then kidnap my baby."

He really did want to believe this scenario she'd just told him. "All right, let's just say that for now, you've convinced me—"

"Let's," Serena agreed, a semblance of a relieved smile curving her mouth.

There were other avenues to explore regarding the foiled kidnapping. For now, he went that route. "Do you have any enemies who would want to get back at you by kidnapping Lora?"

"I'm sorry to disappoint you but I don't have any enemies, period," she told him. "At least," she qualified, "none that I'm aware of."

Given her personality, he tended to believe that was true. He tried something else. "How about the baby's father?"

The smile vanished and her face sobered, darkening like a sky just before a winter storm rolled in. "What about him?"

"Would he kidnap Lora?" he asked. "You know, because he wants full custody of her?" He was familiar with cases like that and they left a bad taste in his mouth, but that didn't change the fact that they existed. "If you give me his name and where I can find him, I'll go question him, see if we can rule him out."

"I'll give you his name," she willingly agreed, "At least the one he gave me, but it's an alias," she told him. "And I have no idea where you can find him. Besides, even if you *could* find him, you'd be wasting your time asking him if he tried to kidnap Lora."

"And why is that?" Before she answered him, Carson read between the lines. "You're telling me he doesn't want to be a father?"

Serena's laugh was totally without a drop of humor. "I don't know what he wants to be, other than a full-time thief." She took the dishes over to the sink and began rinsing them.

Carson came up behind her. "You know you're going to have to give me more details than that," he told her.

She didn't look at Carson at first. She just braced her hands against the sink, desperately trying to center herself. "You're not going to be satisfied until you make me wind up spilling my insides to you, are you?"

His tone softened just a little. "I have no interest in your private life, Serena, but there's more at stake here than just your pride," he told her.

Serena closed her eyes for a moment, trying to separate herself from the words she was about to say. And then she turned around to tell Carson what he was waiting to hear.

"I was out of town at one of the region's bigger horse auctions. We were both bidding on the same horses. When I outbid him, he asked if he could buy me a beer to celebrate. A number of beers and whiskeys later, we were in my room, discussing the finer points of a horse's flanks," she said wryly.

"The next morning, I woke up to find that he was gone, along with all the cash in my wallet and my credit cards." She tried her best to keep the edge of bitterness out of her voice, but some of it came through. "I thought that was the worst of it—until three months later when I found that I was pregnant. And, like I said, the name he gave me was an alias so there was no way I could get in touch with him and tell him that he was about to become a father. He probably still doesn't know—and that's fine with me."

Offering comfort had never been something he was good at. Right now, Carson found himself wishing that it was. "I'm sorry."

She raised her eyes to his. "For asking?"

"No," he said honestly, "for what you went through."

That caused her to instantly rally—and grow slightly defensive. "Don't be. Lora's the most important person in my life and if I hadn't gone through all that, she wouldn't be here. She's my silver lining."

He took his cue from that. "I'm sure she is. And I'm going to keep you both safe." He said it matter-of-factly, but it was a promise, one that he intended to stand by.

"Thank you for that," she told him, her voice growing a little raspy. "If I ever lost her, I don't know what I'd do or how I'd ever recover from that."

The very thought of that happening caused tears to form in her eyes. Serena was immediately embarrassed about being so vulnerable in front of someone, especially in front of the detective.

"Sorry, you don't need to have me carrying on like a hysterical female. Go about doing whatever you're supposed to be doing," she told him, turning away so Carson wouldn't see the tears that she couldn't seem to stop from falling.

He stood there for a moment, watching her shoulders as they moved ever so slightly. He knew she was crying, and he hated that he had inadvertently caused that. He was torn between pretending he didn't notice and trying, ineptly, to comfort her.

But he was afraid that if he took her into his arms, strictly to comfort her, something of an entirely different nature might result.

However, he couldn't bring himself to just callously walk out, either. So he plucked a napkin from the napkin holder on the table and handed it to her.

"Thought you might need this," he murmured as he and Justice left the room.

Carson and his canine partner made the rounds on the ranch, covering the perimeter outside the mansion first. Urging Justice over to where the would-be kidnapper had jumped from Serena's balcony, he had the canine carefully survey the entire area, looking for a scent that would lead the dog to find whoever had made the inept attempt.

Justice suddenly became alert, finding a scent and eagerly following it for approximately a quarter of a mile where the scent, from the K-9's reaction, began to fade. Right next to a set of tire tracks.

Carson cursed under his breath, frustrated. Whoever the kidnapper was, he'd apparently made his escape via some sort of vehicle. Most likely a Jeep from the looks of them, he guessed.

The Jeep had driven onto a gravel road several yards away and that was where both the tire tracks and the scent abruptly ended.

Justice moved around in circles, looking as frustrated as he felt, Carson thought.

"You did your best, Justice," he told the dog. "But if the guy's stupid enough to come back, we'll be ready for him and he can kiss his sorry butt goodbye."

It occurred to Carson as he continued covering the grounds, looking for another lead or clue, that he was no longer referring to the person who had invaded Serena's home as "she."

"How about that?" he muttered to himself.

He supposed that Serena had finally won him over. Despite the necklace and the name written beside his brother's body, he was beginning to consider that Demi Colton was not behind any of this. Maybe Serena was right.

Maybe someone *was* trying to frame her.

With Demi out of the running—for now, he qualified—that brought him back to square one and a world full of possible suspects.

Carson dug in.

He spent the rest of the day questioning ranch hands to see if any of them had heard or seen anything last night that could help him identify who the potential kidnapper was.

As he'd expected, none of the hands had anything in the way of positive information to offer. The one thing he came away with was that they all sounded as if they were eager to help. They all seemed to like Serena.

"Hell, she doesn't treat us like we're dirt under her fingernails, like her mama does," one of the hands, Jake Rowan, confided when he was out of Anders's earshot.

"She's fine with working right alongside of us," Ramon Del Campo, another hand, told Carson. "You need anything to help find whoever took that shot at her, you let us know."

Carson nodded. For the most part, he'd found that when civilian volunteers got involved, things became more dangerous, not less. But wanting to foster this display of goodwill, he made a point of thanking each of the ranch hands before moving on.

During the course of the day, while conducting the interviews, Carson also checked in a number of times on Serena. She was working with the horses in the stable and the corral under the watchful eyes of several ranch hands at any one time. It put his mind somewhat at ease about her welfare.

Carson also stopped at the house to make sure that Lora was safe. Alma seemed capable enough, but the housekeeper, although quite sturdy, wouldn't be a match for anyone who chose to overpower her. Carson directed a couple of the ranch hands to keep watch outside the house, both front and back. They had instructions to fire off a round to get his attention in case someone they didn't know tried to get into the house.

Dusk was just setting in and he was bone tired as he walked into the mansion. Serena was in the living room, sitting on the sofa with Lora on her lap.

"So how are you?" Carson asked, crossing over to her.

"Tired. Why?" Serena asked warily. It was obvious that she thought he was about to spring something on her.

Carson shrugged, thinking that maybe he shouldn't have said anything. But he had had enough of isolating himself the way he'd been doing these last few years. A man shouldn't have to live like that, he silently argued.

He forced himself to continue. "It's just that when I left this morning, you seemed kind of upset. I just want you to know that I wasn't trying to pry."

He definitely wasn't the kind to pry, Serena thought. If anything, he was the kind to encourage building up barricades. Barricades kept him safe from making any personal contact.

"I know that," she said.

Carson forced himself to go on. "I just wanted to rule out the possibility of Lora's father kidnapping her, either for the ransom or because he just wanted custody of the baby."

"I know that, too," she replied quietly. She didn't want to talk about what amounted to a one-night stand. "Could we change the subject?"

He wasn't finished yet. "In a minute."

Annoyed, she asked, "What else do you want to ask me?"

"Right now, nothing," he answered. "I just felt that since I burrowed into your life, making you uncomfortable, I should tell you something about mine so we're on equal footing."

She didn't quite understand where this was going, but she felt she had to tell him that, "I have no desire to make you feel uncomfortable."

"Yeah, well, then, maybe I feel that I owe this to

you," he said. This was hard for him, but he felt he needed to share this with someone and if anyone would understand what he'd gone through, it would be Serena. "Just listen, okay?"

"Okay," she agreed, hoping he wasn't about to tell her something that she was going to regret hearing. "Talk."

Chapter 16

Carson thought of sitting down before he spoke, then decided that he would rather be on his feet when he told Serena what he had been keeping to himself for such a long time.

For some inexplicable reason, standing made him feel less vulnerable and more in control of a situation.

The silence began to deepen.

It is now or never, he told himself.

"I was in a relationship—" he began slowly.

"'Was' or 'are'?" Serena wanted to know.

Despite the fact that she was having feelings for him, it occurred to her that she had no idea about Carson's actual personal life, knew nothing about him at all outside of the fact that he worked for her brother. If Carson had someone in his life, she needed to know now, before anything went any further.

Before her feelings went any deeper.

She'd been blindsided by a good-looking man before and she didn't intend for that to ever happen to her again. Carson might be here at the mansion for the sole purpose of keeping her and Lora safe, which was quite admirable of him, but that still didn't mean that the man wasn't out to further his own personal agenda.

"Was," Carson told her, stressing the word. "Her name was Lisa," he added, knowing that Serena, like most women, would want to know that. "We were starting to get really serious when she told me that she was pregnant."

Haunted by her own memories, Serena's back automatically went up. "Let me guess, you dropped her like a hot potato."

"No," Carson replied, then further surprised her by saying, "I asked her to marry me, but she wouldn't. Said she needed time so that she could work some things out."

"And?" Serena asked, fully expecting Carson to tell her that he then had his own second thoughts and used the time to make his getaway.

"She took a *really* long time thinking," he continued stoically, "and while she was doing all this thinking, the baby decided to come early. Lisa went into premature labor." There was a great deal of emotion brimming in his voice as he told her, even though he was doing his best to keep that emotion at bay. "I didn't find out until after the fact."

Serena grew very quiet, waiting for him to finish his story. At this point, she no longer knew what to think or where this was going. All she knew was that he sounded extremely sad.

Carson avoided looking at her. "I got to the hospital just before Lisa died," he said quietly.

"I'm so sorry." Moved, Serena reached over and covered his hand with hers in an effort to offer comfort. "And the baby?"

"It was a girl." His eyes met hers. "She died the next day."

Serena felt her heart twisting in her chest. For a moment, she couldn't even breathe. "Carson—"

He shrugged away her pity and whatever condolences she was trying to convey.

"These things happen," he told her gruffly. "I didn't tell you this to get your pity. Since you felt I was digging into your life, I wanted to tell you something about mine so that you didn't feel like you were the only one who was exposed." He nodded toward the baby. "I think you'd better get her up to her room," he told her. "She's asleep."

"In a moment," Serena answered.

She rose to her feet and placed Lora in the cradle by the sofa, then walked over to Carson. She had sworn to herself that she had absolutely no time for any meaningless dalliances with men. As far as she was concerned, her life was full just the way it was, with her daughter and her work. Good-looking men were nothing but trouble.

But there was something in Carson Gage's eyes that not only moved her, it spoke to her.

As he was telling her about his unsuccessful relationship and the newborn who had died, even though he'd tried to turn away, she'd seen indescribable pain in his eyes. That was something that couldn't be faked.

She found herself pushing aside her own situation, her own barriers, and wanting to comfort him. At least that was what she told herself.

Before she could think it through, she'd moved closer to Carson and in the next heartbeat, she found herself raising her face up to his and kissing him.

Everything became blurry.

She wasn't even sure if Carson met her halfway or if he had just stood very, very still and allowed her to make the final move.

All she knew was one moment her heart was reaching out to him, the next her mouth was sealed to his.

But while she might have started the kiss, Carson certainly completed it.

His arms went around her, drawing her even closer to him as the kiss deepened to the point that she felt as if she was falling headlong down into a wide, bottomless abyss.

She caught herself clinging to him, trying to keep the room from spinning so fast that she lost her balance. So fast that she lost all perspective.

Carson was the one who ended the kiss, drawing back from her.

She looked at him in dazed surprise.

His pulse was racing faster than the car he'd once taken for a joyride years ago. Part of him, the part that belonged to the reckless teen he'd once been, wanted to take her right here and make love to her. Wanted her so badly, he physically ached.

But he wasn't that reckless teenager anymore, he was a police detective with responsibilities. That meant that he couldn't allow his desires, no matter how strong they were, to dictate his behavior.

Taking hold of Serena's shoulders, he looked into her eyes. "You don't want to do this," he told her.

Serena's heart was hammering so hard, she found that she could hardly breathe. With slow, measured words, she told Carson, "I'm only going to say this once. I'm going to go upstairs to put the baby to bed. After that, I'm going to my room. If you want me, you know where to find me."

She wasn't sure exactly how she managed to walk over to the cradle. It almost felt like she was having an out-of-body experience. She could see herself doing it. Her legs felt so wobbly, she was certain she'd collapse on the floor before she got to the baby.

But she didn't collapse. She made it to the baby's cradle.

Digging deep for strength, Serena picked Lora up in her arms.

With the sleeping baby cradled in her arms and operating on what amounted to automatic pilot, she went to the staircase and slowly made her way up the stairs. All the while, Serena kept praying for two things: that the baby would go on sleeping and that Carson would come upstairs.

Reaching the nursery, she went in and very gently placed her daughter down in the crib. She stood there for a moment, watching Lora sleep. Then, leaving the door between the two rooms opened just a crack, she tiptoed out again and went into her own bedroom.

Her hands were actually shaking as she shed her clothes and then slipped on a nightgown. It was her favorite nightgown, a soft, light blue garment that looked and felt as if it had been spun out of gossamer angel wings.

She looked down at the nightgown. *That's it, Serena. Play hard to get. You're going to wind up with gooseflesh, waiting for a man who isn't going to show up.*

Her heart stopped the very moment she heard the light rap on her door. The roof of her mouth felt so dry, she could barely get the two words out.

"Come in."

The next moment, the door slowly opened and then Carson slipped into the room. He closed the door behind him but made no move to come closer.

Instead, he remained where he was, as if second thoughts had immobilized him.

But he wasn't having second thoughts. He was looking at Serena. His gaze washed slowly over her. She looked like a vision.

Serena was standing next to her bed. The light she'd left on shone right through her nightgown, leaving very little to the imagination.

His imagination took flight anyway.

Carson had no idea how he didn't wind up swallowing his own tongue.

"It's cold tonight. You're going to wind up freezing to death," he told her in a voice that was so low, it was hardly audible.

"Not if I find a way to keep warm," Serena answered him.

Was he going to turn away? Had she made a terrible mistake? She refused to allow her mind to go there.

Her eyes never left Carson's face, waiting for him to make a move. Praying it was the right one.

And then, because he could resist her for only so long, because he needed what Serena was offering him, needed it not just physically but emotionally as well, he cut the distance between them and swept her up in his arms.

This was wrong and he knew it, but he just couldn't help himself. "I should have my head examined," he whispered.

"Later," she said just before she brought her mouth up to his.

His last ounce of resistance disappeared, evaporating in the heat that had just flared up between them as her body pressed up against his.

Any last efforts he might have put forth to talk her out of what they were about to do vanished, burned away to a crisp as one kiss mushroomed into another.

And another.

It was hard for him to say which of them was more eager for this to happen. Up until now, he'd thought of himself as a tower of restraint. But faced with her eager mouth trailing along his face, his neck, his throat, restraint shattered into more pieces than he could ever possibly count.

When Lisa had died, followed by the death of their daughter, Carson had felt like a man who had been literally gutted. He became merely a shell of a man who was just going through the motions of pretending to still be alive. He walked, he talked, he got things done, but he simply didn't feel.

Not a single thing.

But now, tonight, with Serena in his arms like

this, he felt as if he had suddenly been brought back from the dead.

And it felt incredibly wonderful to realize that he was alive.

Carson couldn't remember stripping off his clothes. There was a vague awareness that Serena had helped, but he couldn't say that for sure. All he knew was that the clothes had been in his way and he'd got free of them as quickly as possible.

The diaphanous web that Serena'd had on was discarded as well, becoming a shimmering, barely blue heap on the floor next to his clothes.

Then there was nothing left between them except for unresolved passion.

Pulling her against him, Carson exulted in the intoxicating feel of Serena's bare skin heating against his.

His hands traveled along the length of her body, caressing, stroking, glorying in the softness that had him all but drunk with desire.

He made love to her a hundred different ways, his lips trailing along the curves and swells of her supple form, lingering over her breasts, her hips, working his way slowly down to the very core of her.

When she suddenly gasped and reared, grabbing hold of the comforter beneath her and all but shredding it, Carson lingered longer. He used his tongue, his lips and his very breath to bring her up and over into a climax that had her biting her lip to keep from crying out his name and waking up the baby.

When he moved up along her body again, Serena was all but numb for a moment.

And then, as if suddenly infused by a bolt of sheer energy crafted out of her ecstasy, Serena reversed their positions, straddling him. Working magic she hadn't known that, until this very moment, she was capable of.

With carefully calculated movements, she teased his body until she managed to bring him close to the brink of fulfillment.

Carson caught her hand, stilling it. Then, with his eyes on hers, he switched their positions again until he was over her.

His eyes holding her prisoner, he parted her legs and entered.

But where she expected an overpowering thrust, Carson delivered a gentle, determined one instead. The thrusts became magnified and increased with every movement thereafter until they were both moving so fast, she found herself as breathless as he was.

They raced up the steep incline together, silently focused on mutual satisfaction.

She clung tightly to him and then it happened. The final plunge that sent them into a star-filled euphoria that exploded, then embraced them as the stars showered down around them.

Her heart was pounding so incredibly hard, Serena didn't think she was going to be able to ever catch her breath again, to ever have her heart slow down to a decent rate.

It didn't matter. At that moment, it didn't matter. If this was the way she was going to exit the world, so be it.

And then, slowly, the world came back into focus. The room took on form and dimensions, and just like that, she was back in her bed again.

Back in her bed but not alone.

Serena knew she should say something, but she didn't want to.

Not yet.

Right now, all she wanted to do was lie there and feel the heat of his body mingling with hers, feel his heart hammering as hard as hers.

Listen to the sound of his ragged breathing as it echoed hers.

Later there would be time for all the other things. For words and for the inevitable regrets that were bound to follow in their wake.

But right now, at this very moment, she wanted to pretend that she lived in a perfect world and that every glorious thing that had happened just now would continue to happen.

Given enough time.

As his euphoria slowly dissolved, he realized that Serena was being extremely quiet. Had he hurt her?

Had she gone into some kind of shock over what had just happened between them?

Or was that fear that had immobilized both her tongue and her body this way?

Carson wanted to reassure her. To say something to make her feel better about what had just transpired between them—something that he thought was wonderful—but for the life of him, he didn't know how.

So for now, he chose to take the easy out.

He remained silent, just listening to her breathe.

And wishing that there was a way to make this moment last if not forever, then at least for a long, long time.

Chapter 17

She was alone.

Serena could sense it even before she opened her eyes to verify if that the sinking feeling in the pit of her stomach was true.

Carson had gone.

After a night of what she felt was the most incredible lovemaking she had ever experienced, Carson had slipped out of her bed while she was asleep, disappearing from her room without a word.

Exactly the way that the man who had fathered Lora had done.

Disappointment raked long, sharp fingernails across Serena's soul, scarring her. Making her want to throw things.

Making her want to cry.

She rubbed the heel of her hand against her eyes, wiping away tears before they had a chance to fall. How could she have been so stupid, so wrong about someone? Yet here she was, alone in bed, so there was no other conclusion left for her to draw except that Carson was just like every other male on the face of the earth: self-centered.

He had seen his opportunity and he'd taken it without a single qualm.

Serves you right for being such a blind idiot, Serena upbraided herself. *Now, just stop feeling sorry for yourself and get over it!* she silently ordered. *You've got a baby depending on you, that's the only thing that matters here.*

The second she thought of her daughter, Serena realized that Lora had been unusually quiet during the night. Was there something wrong? Or had the housekeeper got up early and gone to the nursery to look after the baby?

She's a better mother than I am, Serena thought, feeling ashamed of herself. She should have been thinking about Lora, not about her own long-suppressed needs and desires.

What was wrong with her? she silently demanded, annoyed with herself.

Kicking aside her covers, Serena suddenly realized that she still had nothing on. Swearing softly, she grabbed a robe in lieu of a nightgown and quickly made her way to the nursery.

Softly opening the door so as not to wake her daughter on the outside chance that Lora actually *was* asleep, Serena looked into the room.

And stopped dead.

Carson was sitting in the rocking chair with Lora in his arms, quietly rocking her. Not only that, but he was feeding the baby a bottle. He'd obviously found one of the formula bottles that were kept in the miniature refrigerator for just these sort of midnight feedings. She'd put them there so that there'd be no need to go all the way down to the kitchen while she was half-asleep. A bottle warmer stood on the counter and she could see that it had been pressed into use, as well.

Justice lay on the floor right in front of Carson's feet. The German shepherd had raised his head the moment she walked in, alerting Carson to her presence.

When he looked at her over his shoulder, Serena asked, "What are you doing?"

It absolutely stunned her at how very right this incredibly domestic scene seemed.

"Lora was hungry. I didn't want her to wake you up, so I got a bottle to feed her," Carson answered simply.

If he knew Lora was hungry, she must have been

crying. Guilt took a bite out of her. She should have been up at the first whimper.

"How did I not hear her crying?" she asked, puzzled.

"I think probably because you were pretty exhausted at the time," Carson told her, his voice low, soothing.

She knew he didn't mean it this way, but she felt patronized. "And you weren't?" she challenged.

Was Carson saying that even though he'd worn her out, he was still full of energy and ready to go? In either case it seemed that of the two of them, he made a better mother than she did.

"I'm used to sleeping with one eye and one ear open, remember?" he reminded her. "I heard Lora stirring and making noises, so I figured it was just a matter of time before she'd start crying. I thought you might appreciate sleeping in for a change. My guess is that you haven't had a decent night's sleep in a while now."

He talked as if he knew what new mothers went through. Pretty insightful for a man who had never been married, she thought.

"I haven't," she admitted, staring at him as if he had just suddenly acquired a halo.

This, to her, was almost better than the night they had just spent together. That had been wondrous, but this spoke of a type of kindness that she knew wasn't all that common. It touched her heart in ways that their lovemaking hadn't.

Serena roused herself before she melted completely. "I'd better change her," she said, moving closer to take Lora from him.

He rose but not to turn the baby over to her. Lora had fallen asleep midfeeding, and he wanted to place her in her crib.

"Already taken care of," he said.

He was telling her that he had actually changed Lora's diaper. She stared at Carson again, stunned speechless.

Finding her tongue, she said, "I don't believe you."

"The old diaper's in the covered pail," he told her, nodding to the container next to the changing table. "You can check if you want to."

Serena was almost tempted to do just that. Pressing her lips together, she could only shake her head in wonder. "How did you—"

He grinned. "It's not exactly rocket science, and despite what you might think, I'm not an idiot. Disposable diapers, wipes, lotion, a secured place to do the changing and voilà," Carson rattled off in a low whisper. "No big mystery."

He placed the sleeping baby back into her crib and quietly withdrew from the nursery.

Leaving the door open just a crack as he entered Serena's suite, he turned toward her. "When

I was with Lora just now, I had a chance to do some thinking."

He was about to tell her what had occurred to him while he'd been rocking and feeding Lora, but he never got the chance. Because the moment he'd turned toward her, Serena threw her arms around him and sealed her mouth to his in an expression of utter gratitude.

Whatever he was going to say was lost for the next hour as they once again became reacquainted with just how very in sync they were with one another.

Lovemaking begot lovemaking.

Finally, tottering on the edge of exhaustion, they lay next to one another, wrapped in the last fragments of soul-comforting euphoria. Carson drew her a little closer to him.

He was in total awe of how she seemed to be able to unlock all these feelings within him, feelings that had him wanting to protect her and her baby, not just as a member of the police department, but as a man. A man who hadn't realized just how very lonely and alone he'd been until last night.

So, with one arm tightly around her, he stroked Serena's hair, content to remain that way for as long as humanly possible.

That was exactly the moment that Serena chose to raise her head from his chest and look up into his eyes. "You said something about you thinking of something while you were feeding Lora. What was it?"

It took him a moment to recreate that moment. Making love with Serena had a way of clouding his brain and making everything else vanish.

And then he remembered. "A while back you mentioned something about seeing the Larson brothers riding around on your ranch."

She recalled the incident perfectly, as well as the cold shiver that had gone down her spine. "They were. They told Anders that they were thinking about getting their own place and just wanted to take a look around ours."

"Did you believe them?" He thought he knew the answer to that, given her tone of voice, but he just wanted to be sure.

"No," she retorted with feeling. Rising above the last of the intoxicating feeling that making love with Carson had created, she was now focused on telling him about how she'd felt seeing the Larsons skulking around her ranch. "I couldn't shake the feeling that they were somehow casing the Double C Ranch. You know, getting the lay of the land, things like that."

Carson filled in what she wasn't saying. "So a kidnapper would know what he was up against and which way he needed to go to make a quick getaway once he had the baby."

The very thought filled her with horror. Serena was fully alert now and sitting up. She put into words what he hadn't said yet. "Do you think one of them tried to kidnap Lora?"

He'd already discarded that idea—in part. "Probably too risky for one of them to make the actual attempt. They don't like putting themselves on the line like that. But that doesn't mean they wouldn't send someone else to do it."

He saw Serena's eyes widen and he wished he didn't have to be the one to tell her this. But he knew she wasn't the type who wanted to be kept in the dark. Serena was better off being made aware of all the possibilities.

"Your father's a powerful man around here, Serena, not to mention wealthy. Kidnapping Judson Colton's grandchild would mean a fast payoff for the Larsons." He could see that he'd struck a nerve and he was quick to reassure her. "Don't worry, I'm not going to let anything happen to you or to Lora."

She wanted him to focus on Lora, not her. "I can take care of myself, Carson," she told him. "But you can't be everywhere, and Lora's just a baby."

"How do you feel about protective custody?" he wanted to know. "I can have one of the K-9 officers take her to an undisclosed location and watch over her."

"And Alma," Serena added. "I want Alma to go with Lora."

"You would be the more logical choice to go with Lora," Carson pointed out.

"I know," she admitted, but she just couldn't indulge herself that way. She had responsibilities here, as well. Responsibilities to the ranch. "But Anders can't watch over everything on the ranch on his own. Besides, I can't just abandon the horses. As much as I hate to think about this, there's no telling just how long it'll take you to find this would-be kidnapper," she said. And then she added hopefully, "Maybe you scared him off and he's long gone by now."

He shook his head. "We can't count on that. I'll call Finn and tell him that you've agreed to protective custody—for Lora," he added quickly when he saw the protest rise to her lips. "He'll have one of the detectives come out to the ranch and pick up Lora and your housekeeper," he said. "Meanwhile, I suggest you go tell Alma that she's in for a change of scenery for the time being."

Serena was already up and slipping her robe back on. She quickly crossed back to the nursery in order to get together some things for Lora to use for her protective custody stay.

"Alma loves the baby," she told Carson just as she was about to leave the room. "She'll go anywhere if it means keeping Lora safe."

When he made no answer, she turned around to look at Carson, but he had already left her suite.

"Man moves like smoke," she murmured, shaking her head.

She focused on packing a suitcase for Lora.

* * *

Carson admitted to himself that he was operating purely on a hunch. The other day he'd searched only some of the ranch hands' studio apartments, the ones that had been opened to him. But there were other living quarters that he hadn't looked into. At the time, he had been strictly searching for some sign of Demi.

But now, since he believed that perhaps the Larson brothers were somehow involved in this unsavory business, he needed to look through all the ranch hands' quarters, looking for anything that might connect the brothers to the botched kidnapping attempt and/or the equally unsuccessful attempt on Serena's life.

He was keenly aware of the fact that he had a myriad of questions and so far, no answers, but he had nothing to lose by pushing ahead with this search.

Because the ranch hands were working on the ranch that belonged to Judson Colton, they had no right to an expectation of privacy. They had all signed contracts to that effect when they came to work on the Double C; the thinking being that if any of the ranch hands decided to take it into their heads to steal something—anything at all—from the ranch, a search of their living quarters would be conducted at any time to find it.

So, after telling Anders what he was about to do and with Justice beside him, Carson went from studio apartment to studio apartment, meticulously searching through everything. It was a case of "I'll know it when I see it" since he had no idea just what he was looking for. He just knew that he needed *something* that would help him connect one of the ranch hands to the Larsons.

For the most part, the search wound up being an uneventful parade of one small messy studio apartment after another. They all looked depressingly alike to him, yielding nothing.

He was close to giving up when Justice suddenly came to life in the next to last studio apartment they entered. The canine barked several times and began trying to dig his way under the ranch hand's bed.

Carson got down on his belly and, snaking his way under the bed, he found nothing but dust bunnies for his trouble.

"Nothing here, boy," he said, getting back up again and dusting off his knees.

But Justice kept barking.

"Really wish you could talk, Justice," Carson said. "It would make my life a lot easier."

On a hunch, since Justice continued barking at the bed, Carson lifted the mattress up off the box springs. There were a number of large sealed plastic packets tucked between the two pieces that made up the twin bed.

"Well, what do you know? Sorry I doubted you,

boy," he said, gathering up all the packets from their so-called hiding place.

"Hey, what do you think you're doing?" Pete Murphy, a tall, skinny cowboy demanded as he came into the studio apartment behind Carson. "That's my stuff!"

By now there were seven large packets on the floor and Justice was circling the lot, growing more and more agitated.

Carson squatted down to examine one of the packets more closely. "Are you dealing drugs, Pete?" he asked the cowboy.

"Am I— What? Dealing drugs?" he repeated, his voice cracking in the middle. "No, those are mine. For me," he emphasized.

Carson held up the packet he'd been examining. "Are you trying to tell me that you take these for 'recreational' purposes?"

"Yeah, right. Recreational purposes, that's it. Now, give them back!" he demanded, trying to take possession of the packets that were closest to him.

Rising, Carson looked into the ranch hand's eyes, pinning him in place. "You're selling these for the Larsons, aren't you? How much are they cutting you in for?"

"I don't know what you're talking about," the cowboy denied. "They're not cutting me in for anything."

Which meant that the brothers probably had something on the cowboy that they were holding over his head, Carson thought. "You tried to kidnap Serena Colton's baby, didn't you?"

"Kidnap the baby?" Murphy stuttered, growing visibly frightened. "No, I wouldn't do something like that!"

Carson continued to press, "You certainly match the description of the kidnapper who broke into Serena Colton's suite, trying to steal her baby."

Murphy was sweating now. "You're out of your mind! Okay, maybe I do a little business on the side for the Larsons, but it's strictly the drugs—working out here is hard, damn it, and a man can't be faulted for wanting to take the edge off once in a while. But kidnapping? Hell, no way!"

The cowboy suddenly turned and ran, leaving behind the drugs and everything else in his quarters.

For a split second, Carson debated giving chase, but the cowboy was moving pretty fast. Carson decided that it wasn't worth working up a sweat. Instead, he looked down at Justice. The canine was so well trained, he refrained from running after the cowboy until told to do so.

Carson gave his partner the go-ahead.

"Justice, fetch!" was all he had to say. It was the key phrase he used to train the K-9 to stop someone from fleeing the scene.

Murphy got approximately ten feet beyond his studio apartment before the German shepherd caught hold of his boot and brought him down. Justice pinned the cowboy to the ground with the force of his weight.

"Justice, off!" Carson ordered as he calmly walked up to the fallen cowboy. Murphy began to scramble up to his feet, most likely intending to run again. "I wouldn't do that if I were you," Carson advised quietly.

Murphy froze, fearfully eyeing Justice. To anyone watching, it appeared that the German shepherd was eyeing him in return.

Carson took out his handcuffs.

Chapter 18

"Then it's over," Serena said, breathing a sigh of relief.

It felt as if a huge weight had been taken off her shoulders. Carson had sought her out in the stables after he had returned from town, specifically from the police station where he had taken Pete Murphy. The cowboy had been placed under arrest for possession of cocaine with the intent to sell.

Serena was overjoyed when Carson told her about the arrest. "This means that I can bring Lora back to the ranch."

It had only been less than a day since she'd handed her daughter over to the police detective who had taken the baby into protective custody, but it felt as if it had been weeks.

Carson frowned. He hated doing this to Serena, but in all good conscience, he had to. Lora couldn't be allowed to be brought home yet.

"Not so fast," he warned.

She was ready to have Carson take her to wherever her daughter was being held. Her heart sank when he just stood there.

"Why not?" she wanted to know. "You got the guy, right?"

"I'm not so sure about that."

"But those drugs you found in his room tie Murphy to the Larsons," Serena cried. "They're drug dealers. He's working for them."

Carson shook his head. He'd spent two hours interrogating the cowboy, but he'd got nowhere and it frustrated him.

"Murphy claims that he's not working for anyone, that he just bought those drugs from a dealer to sell on his own. He swears he's not working for the Larsons and that he doesn't know anything about a kidnapping."

"But he's lying, right?" Serena cried desperately. "You told me that the Larsons' thugs are afraid of testifying against them. This could just be another example of that."

He felt for her. He knew exactly what she was going through, but that still didn't change anything. "They are, and I've got no doubt that Murphy is selling drugs for the two brothers. I also wouldn't put it past the Larsons to try to steal a wealthy family's baby just to ransom it back to them—"

Serena didn't let him finish. "So I can't bring Lora home yet."

"Not until I get some proof of that," he continued, determined to get his point across even though it really aggravated him to be the bearer of bad news. "I can't charge Murphy with kidnapping, and as much as I would like to, I can't charge the Larsons with conspiracy to kidnap or anything of the kind."

Disappointment spread out all through Serena. She felt as if she was caught up in a nightmare. She wanted to keep Lora safe, but she missed her daughter more than she thought possible.

"So you're telling me that it's *not* over," she concluded, exasperated beyond words.

"Not yet. But soon," he added quickly. "I promise, soon. Until then, Lora's safe and I'm going to keep you safe, as well. And to make sure nothing happens to you, I'm going to have Detective Saunders stay with you," he told her, mentioning another member of the K-9 team. "I'm leaving Justice here with you, too."

Serena had an uneasy feeling he was telling her that he wasn't going to be around. She looked at him suspiciously. "Why? Where are you going?"

"I just got a call from Bo's lawyer, Jonathan Witherspoon," Carson answered. "He told me that he's going to be reading Bo's will to his heirs this afternoon, and I feel I need to be there."

"Out of respect, or because you think he left you something?" Serena wanted to know.

He laughed shortly. He'd long since lost all respect for Bo, and he knew without being told that he wasn't in his brother's will. He had a different reason for attending the reading.

"Neither," he answered. "I want to see who else turns up at the reading and if there are any 'surprises' in the will. Maybe that'll give me some kind of a lead as to who might have actually killed my brother."

She looked at Carson, taking solace where she could find it. "So you don't think it's Demi anymore," she assumed.

He knew how much that meant to Serena and if he was being perfectly honest with himself, he was beginning to have suspicions that someone actually *had* tried to frame Serena's cousin.

"Let's just say I'm more open to other possibilities," he answered.

Serena nodded. She didn't care how he phrased it just as long as he stopped obsessing that Demi was the one who had killed his brother. "Good. What time's the reading of the will?"

"Two o'clock." Carson looked at her, his curiosity aroused. "Why?"

She was already stripping her leather gloves off. "Give me half an hour, and I'll get ready," she said, already halfway out of the stable.

Carson still didn't understand. "Why?" he asked again.

"Because I'm going with you," she answered Carson simply.

Maybe she'd misunderstood him. "There's no need for you to go—" he began.

Carson had been the one to discover his brother's body and since then, she knew that Carson had gone through a lot, even though he kept it all bottled up. She didn't want Carson sitting through the reading of the will by himself. Who knew what emotions he'd wind up dealing with? She wanted to be there for him, to let him know, even silently, that he wasn't alone.

However, she knew that if she began to explain any of this, he would just balk at her reasons. Most likely he'd just tell her to stay here.

Knowing that the detective appreciated minimalism, she merely told him, "Yes, there is," and hoped he'd leave it at that.

Carson was about to argue with her, to insist that there was no reason for him to drag her to the reading. He wouldn't be going himself if Bo had died in his sleep at some ripe old age. There'd be no reason to go then. It was Bo's murder that was forcing him to attend this reading like some undercover voyeur.

Given that, he reconsidered and grudgingly admitted that he needed to have her with him. So he sighed and echoed, "Half an hour," as if putting her on notice that he would wait half an hour and no more. He wanted her to believe that if she took longer, he'd just leave without her—even though he knew he'd wind up waiting for her anyway.

As it turned out, he didn't have to wait.

"Five minutes to spare," Serena told him proudly, sliding into the passenger seat of his car. She looked in the rear of the vehicle and saw that Justice was already in the car. They had *both* been waiting for her to come out. "Is he going to the reading, as well?" she asked. The question was asked only partially tongue in cheek.

"I'm on duty," he told her. "I don't go anywhere without Justice."

Leaning back, she put her hand out for the dog to sniff, then petted his head. "Does the lawyer know you're bringing a 'friend'?"

"I don't think Witherspoon'll mind my bringing you," Carson said, starting up his vehicle.

He didn't fool her, she thought. He knew perfectly well that she was referring to the K-9. But she said it anyway.

"I was referring to Justice. This is a will reading. Mr. Witherspoon might not be prepared to have a German shepherd 'attend' the reading."

"Justice goes wherever I go," he told her matter-of-factly. "We're a team."

"I know that," she said, petting the dog again, "but

some people might not be comfortable having a big German shepherd so close to them."

Carson met her observation with a shrug. "Well, that's their problem, not mine," he told her. "Besides, if they don't have anything to hide, everything'll be all right."

Serena settled back into her seat. "This should be interesting," she said, bracing herself for what the next hour or so held.

Jonathan Witherspoon looked as if he had been born wearing a three-piece suit with a matching shirt and tie. The two or three times that Carson had crossed paths with the lawyer, he got the impression that the word *casual* had no meaning for the tall, angular man who looked at the world through thick, rimless glasses. Sporting prematurely gray hair since he had turned thirty-five, the lawyer was only now approaching the age where his gray hair finally suited him, even though it had begun to thin considerably.

When Carson arrived with Serena for the reading of the will, the folding chairs that Witherspoon had his administrative assistant set up in his office were almost all taken. There were only a few remaining empty seats.

Carson guided Serena in first and took a chair on the aisle so that he could easily hold on to Justice. Specifically, he wanted to see if Justice would react to anyone at the reading. He'd always felt, right from the beginning, that Justice seemed to be able to actually *sense* evil. Carson took himself to task for not having brought the dog with him to the bachelor party, despite being off duty. He might have been able to find the killer right then and there and there would be no need for this elaborate game of hide-and-seek.

Witherspoon drew his shallow cheeks in even more than he usually did when he saw the dog sitting beside Carson. The lawyer looked none too pleased about the four-footed attendee, but apparently knew better than to say anything to Carson. He only scowled.

Looking around, Carson noted that Bo's ex-wife, Darby, was seated all the way in the back. Hayley, Bo's fiancée was front and center, just as he had expected her to be. As he watched, she turned around twice to shoot dirty looks at Darby.

This, he thought, was really shaping up to be a very interesting afternoon.

Leaning in closer to Serena, he whispered, "You sure you want to be here?"

"You're here, so I'm here," she told him. "Besides," she added, keeping her voice low, "this makes me realize why I like working with horses so much more than working with people."

Carson suppressed a laugh.

The next moment, Witherspoon cleared his throat

rather loudly, indicating that they should all stop talking and pay attention to what he was about to say.

"All right, it looks like we're all here," the lanky lawyer said. He sat down behind his desk as he looked around at the various people who had gathered here in hopes of getting at least a piece of the considerable amount of money that Bo had accrued or, if not that, then a part of his breeding business. "Let's get started, shall we?"

In a monotonous, droning voice that seemed incredibly suited to the lawyer's face and demeanor, Witherspoon read the will in its entirety, stating every single detail that the law required in order for the will to be deemed a binding legal document.

When the lawyer came to the part that everyone had been waiting for—the distribution of Bo's possessions—the reading went far more quickly than anyone had actually anticipated.

"And I leave the entirety of my dog breeding business, as well as my ranch, both located at—" Witherspoon paused to read the address that everyone was well acquainted with, unintentionally stretching out the drama.

Almost everyone in the room had leaned forward. No one wanted to miss a single syllable of this part.

"—to my ex-wife, Darby Gage. I hope that this will make up for some of the things that I put you through, Darby."

"No!" Hayley screamed, all but going into shock.

She jumped to her feet, knocking over the folding chair she'd been sitting in and discarding any and all pretense of grief. "There's got to be some kind of a mistake," she cried glaring accusingly at Witherspoon.

Witherspoon maintained his composure. It was obvious to Serena that the lawyer had to have been the target of angry heirs before Hayley's vitriolic display.

"I assure you that there's no mistake. I was there when Bo signed this." Holding up the last page of the document he'd been reading from, he displayed a seal. "It's been notarized."

"I don't care if it was signed by all the saints in heaven and half of Congress. That piece of paper's a fake! Bo would never have done something like this to me! He wouldn't have given that little scheming witch everything!"

Practically choking on her fury, Hayley gave every indication that she was going to lunge at Darby. Her hands went up and her freshly lacquered nails were outstretched, ready to rake over the ex-wife's face. Carson was immediately on his feet and got between his brother's fiancée and his ex-wife.

Justice growled at the woman, ready to take Hayley down on command. Serena had got to her feet as well, waiting to help Carson if he needed it. Since she was a woman, she felt she could restrain Hayley in ways that Carson couldn't.

But he caught Hayley's hands before she could do any damage.

"Settle down, Hayley," he ordered sternly.

"Settle down?" she shrieked, trying to pull free. "Didn't you just hear what Witherspoon just read? Everything's hers! That miserable liar didn't leave me *anything*!"

The more Hayley struggled, the tighter his grip on her hands grew. "You can get a lawyer and contest the will if you feel this strongly about it," he told her, his voice unnervingly calm.

"I'm not getting a damn lawyer," she spit, then retorted, "There are other ways to resolve this injustice!"

Carson immediately cut her short. "Don't say anything you're going to regret," he warned.

"What I regret is wasting my time with that backstabbing, worthless brother of yours," Hayley cried.

Still watching her carefully, Carson released the woman.

Swinging around, Hayley glared at Witherspoon. "You haven't heard the last of this!" she declared.

With that, she stormed out of the lawyer's office, pausing only long enough to spit on the floor right in front of Darby.

For her part, Darby didn't react. She appeared to be absolutely stunned.

The people sitting near her, many of whom had either been bequeathed a nominal sum of money or had learned that they would be receiving nothing at all, murmured among themselves. They filed out of the lawyer's office one by one, many in a state of disbelief.

In the end, only Carson, Serena and Darby were left with Witherspoon.

"Are you all right?" Carson asked his ex-sister-in-law.

He couldn't quite read the expression on Darby's face. It was a cross between what he took to be utter shock and something like subdued joy. He had the feeling that Darby wasn't quite sure exactly where she was right now.

"Fine," she finally managed to reply. And then, as if coming to, she turned to look at Witherspoon. "Did you just say that Bo left *everything* to me?" she asked in total disbelief.

"Why don't you come over here closer to my desk so I don't have to shout?" the lawyer told her, not that he appeared to be capable of shouting.

Rising from the last row, Darby made her way forward, moving in slow motion like someone who wasn't sure if they were awake or caught up in some sort of a dream.

Still looking dazed, she sat down in the single chair that Witherspoon had facing his desk.

The lawyer raised his tufted gray eyebrows and looked over expectantly toward Carson and the woman who was beside him. "I'm going to have to ask the two of you to leave now. I have several details to discuss with Ms. Gage."

Carson nodded. Bo had managed to drop a bombshell, even in death.

Chapter 19

"Well, certainly didn't see that one coming," Carson commented to Serena.

He was driving them away from Witherspoon's office. For all intents and purposes, Justice appeared to have fallen asleep in the back seat the mo they'd taken off.

"Then Bo and his ex-wife weren't on terms?" Serena asked.

She was totally in the dark about C brother in general beyond the fact owned a breeding business and unit with German shepherds.

"Bo wasn't the type to worr terms with any of his exes.

Carson told her. "I think it's fair to say that he was always only looking out for himself." As far as brothers went, he and Bo were as different as night and day. "Once Bo got what he wanted, he moved on. When he decided that Darby was cramping his style, he shed her like a snake sheds its skin, without so much as a backward glance. When the marriage ended, he only tossed a couple of crumbs her way and by crumbs, I mean literal *crumbs*. Bo gave her a part-time job cleaning kennels at the breeding business they *both* had once owned."

Serena viewed that as pretty callous, but she did always like to think the best of people. "Maybe it was like Bo said in his will. He felt guilty about the way he'd treated her and this was his way of mak-
- it up to Darby."

" " Carson answered, but he was highly
n't nearly that noble. There had to
what he had done.

didn't sound con-
forgery?"

No, the will's real
ntious, he would
itution or switch.

on the dashboard
ow pressed a but-
s's cell. When he
on started talking.

"Chief, it's Gage. I think we just might have ourselves another suspect in my brother's murder," Carson told Serena's brother.

"Make this quick, Gage. I'm in the middle of something right now," Finn prompted. "And this better be something more than just an off-the-wall theory."

There was noise on the other end of the line and Carson couldn't quite make it out, but he knew better than to ask. The chief would tell him what was going on if Finn wanted him to know.

"I was just at the reading of Bo's will," he told Finn.

"And?"

He knew he had to cut to the chase, but he felt certain that this would give the chief pause. "You're never going guess who my brother left his ranch and dog breeding business to."

"Well, it's not you because you would have led with giving me your notice," Finn said impatiently. "And I take it that it's not his fiancée because that was what everyone was expecting. Okay, I'll bite. Who did Bo leave his ranch and business to?"

"Darby Gage, his ex-wife."

For a moment, there was nothing but silence on the other end, as if Finn was trying to make heads or tails out of what he'd just been told.

"You're putting me on," he finally cried. From the sound of his voice, Carson surmised that the chief was as stunned as everyone else at the reading had been. "Seriously?"

"Seriously," Carson confirmed. "You realize what this means, don't you?"

"Yeah, I realize," Finn answered with a heavy sigh. "You're right. We just got ourselves another suspect." He had a question for Carson. "You think your ex-sister-in-law knew she was getting everything?"

Carson told the chief what he'd observed upon coming into the office. "I don't think she even knew she was in the will. From what I gathered, she was only there because Witherspoon told her to be there."

"Well, what do you know," Finn murmured more to himself than to Carson. "This certainly expands our playing field, doesn't it?"

"That's what I was thinking," Carson replied, glad he and Finn were on the same page.

Listening in on Carson's part of the conversation, Serena couldn't hold her tongue any longer.

Raising her voice so that her brother could hear, she said, "Maybe Darby found out about the will and she decided to kill Bo to get her hands on the business—and to pay him back for the way he'd treated her. To cover her tracks, she could have framed Demi for the murder out of spite. You know, as gruesome as it sounds, dipping Bo's finger in his own blood and guiding it to write Demi's name. That way you'd find the blood under his fingernail."

Carson nodded in agreement. That sounded about right to him. "Did you hear that?" he asked, addressing Finn on the cell.

"Is that my sister?" Finn wanted to know. There was a note of confusion in his voice.

"Yeah, she's right here in the car," Carson answered. Knowing Finn wanted more detail, he added, "She insisted on coming to the reading of the will with me."

He heard Finn laugh shortly.

"That's pretty good. Maybe she should be working at the police department instead of with the horses," Finn said.

"No, thank you," Serena said, speaking up. "Horses don't have agendas."

"You want me to bring Darby in for questioning?" Carson asked him.

"No, she's your ex-sister-in-law. You're too close to this," Finn answered. "Let's keep this all above reproach. I'll have Galloway bring her in."

"While you're at it, maybe you should have another go at the 'eyewitness,'" Carson suggested. "It's entirely possible that someone looking to frame Demi paid Paulie Gains off to say that he saw Demi fleeing from the area just before Bo's murder."

"For that matter, if we're considering possibilities, Darby could have put on a red wig and pretended to be Demi as she ran from the crime scene," Serena chimed in.

"Yeah, maybe," Finn agreed. "Anything else happen at the reading, Gage?"

"Yeah, I think you might want to consider putting Darby into protective custody. Bo's fiancée looked like she could have killed Darby with her bare hands once she heard that Darby was inheriting practically everything. Unless you've got any objections, I think I'm going to go and have a word with Hayley, see if she had any clue that this was coming. She looked surprised, but you never know."

"Sure. Go talk to her and get back to me on that," Finn told him.

"Right." As he was about to end the call, a thought occurred to Carson. "Oh, any word on Demi?" he asked.

"There've been a few so-called Demi-sightings in the area, but nothing that panned out. The rest of the team's still out there, looking for her. But now that you've told me about the will, I'm thinking we're going to be changing the focus of our search. At least for the time being. Get back to me if you find out anything," Finn told him again, then terminated the call.

"So we're going to see Hayley?" Serena asked as soon as she heard her brother end the call.

"*I'm* going to see Hayley," Carson corrected. "*After* I take you back to the Double C."

But Serena had other ideas. Now that she'd finally got out, she wanted to help Carson. The sooner all this was resolved, the sooner she could get her daughter back and life could return to normal.

"I think I should come with you," she told him, sounding a lot more confident than he'd anticipated. "Hayley looked like she wanted to kill someone. She won't kill you if there's a witness."

"Or she could kill the witness, too," he pointed out, momentarily indulging in some black humor.

"There's safety in numbers," Serena reminded him. "Besides, I'm not as fragile as I look."

A smile curved his mouth. He thought of the other night. Delicate, yes, but definitely not fragile. Still, out loud he told her, "Good to know."

She got the feeling that he wasn't talking about anything that had to do with Hayley.

They found Bo's former fiancée at home. As they approached her house, they heard the sound of breaking glass and crockery and Hayley yelling at the top of her lungs.

Carson decided to leave Justice in the car for everyone's safety. He didn't want to get the dog unnecessarily agitated. There might be unforeseen consequences of that.

He cracked the windows before turning his attention to the screamfest in Hayley's house.

Still apparently grappling with the huge disappointment she'd just experienced, Hayley Patton was calling Bo every name in the book. And with each name, she hurled another breakable object against the wall.

Carson hesitated and looked at Serena. "Maybe you should stay outside," he told her.

"The hell I will," she countered. "She can't hit both of us at once."

"That's not exactly a consolation," Carson informed her.

The incensed, newly spurned dog trainer's door was unlocked. Carson pushed it open slowly in order not to attract Hayley's attention. He still just narrowly avoided getting hit by a brightly painted vase that smashed into smithereens after a fatal encounter with the wall just beside the door frame.

"Hey!" Carson cried sternly, pushing Serena behind him so she wouldn't get hurt with any flying debris.

Caught up in her rampage, Hayley swung around to face him and glared. "What the hell do you two want?" she demanded angrily, looking as if she was going to hurl the next object at them.

Since Carson was Bo's brother and possibly a target for Hayley's rage, Serena was quick to take the lead and answer the woman's question. "We just came by to see if you're all right."

"All right?" Hayley echoed incredulously. "Of course I'm not all right! I'm the laughingstock of Red Ridge. That no-good, womanizing jackass made me look like a fool in front of everyone I know."

Angry tears came to her eyes. "We were supposed to get married, damn it! Everything was supposed to be mine, not hers! Mine! How could he just give it away to her like that? Like I didn't matter?" Hayley shrieked.

Serena tried to sound as understanding and sympathetic as possible when she asked, "Did Bo ever do or say anything to make you think that he was going to leave it all to Darby?"

Hayley looked at her as if she was crazy. "You think I would have stayed with him if he so much as *hinted* that he was going to do that?" she demanded. "Looks and charm wear pretty thin pretty fast, even Bo's," she told them. "I was in it for the long haul because I thought I'd be taken care of."

Her face darkened as another wave of fury took hold. "Well, he took care of me all right, that dirty, rotten son of a bitch," she cried, picking up another glass and throwing it against the wall.

Carson and Serena moved out of the way as shattered glass flew everywhere.

Carson stayed a few minutes longer, asking Hayley several more questions in between her tirade and the ongoing cavalcade of objects being hurled against the wall and meeting their untimely demise.

It became very clear that as far as knowing that Bo was about to leave the breeding business and his ranch to another woman, Hayley hadn't had a clue.

* * *

When Carson told her he had to make one more stop before they went back to her ranch, Serena thought he wanted to talk to another possible suspect. Either that or he wanted to talk to her brother about Hayley's meltdown in person.

She didn't know what to think when Carson stopped his car in front of a toy store.

"What are we doing here?" she asked as she followed him inside.

The only thing that occurred to her was that he wanted to buy her daughter a toy, but she sincerely doubted that. At three months of age, Lora's favorite playthings were still her fingers and toes. The baby could spend hours just moving them in front of her face, fascinated by the sight.

The answer he gave her caught her off guard. "I want to buy a doll."

Lora was too young for a doll at this point. "Excuse me?"

"I'm buying a doll," he repeated. Caught up in his plan, Carson realized that there was no way Serena could know what he had in mind, so he explained. "I'm looking for one of those lifelike dolls. You know, the ones that look like a real baby." And then he qualified what he meant. "I'm sure this store doesn't carry one of those really specialized ones that I saw advertised in a catalog, the ones that look and feel like a real baby. Some of them even move when you touch them," he said, recalling the description. "I just want one that's about the size of a three-month-old and lifelike enough to fool a kidnapper."

She felt as if her throat was closing up again. There was only one reason he would be doing this. "You think he's coming back, don't you?"

He hated bringing fear back into her life, but she had to understand that there was still a very real danger of her daughter being kidnapped.

"I'm counting on it," he told her. "Because we're going to set a trap for him so that he stops being a threat to you and Lora." He looked at her and saw that she had grown a little pale. He stopped looking up and down the aisles and put his hands on her shoulders, in essence creating a "safe space" for her. "It's the only way, Serena."

"I know," she answered in a hoarse voice.

Pulling herself together, she joined the search for the perfect doll to use as a decoy. Carson was right. Until the would-be kidnapper was caught, she would continue to live in fear for her daughter—and that really wasn't living at all.

"I didn't realize that they could look *this* lifelike," Carson said. They were back in her room at the Double C and he was looking at the doll that had taken them close to an hour to find and cost a great deal more than he'd expected. "Too bad we couldn't have just rented the damn thing," he commented.

He thought of the receipt in his wallet. "These dolls are expensive."

"That's because a lot goes into making one of them. Touch its face," Serena urged.

"Once was enough, thanks." He'd already done that in the store. That was how he'd decided which doll to pick. When he'd picked up the doll from its display, he found that the doll's actual weight felt as if he had a real baby in his arms. It was damn eerie, he thought.

She couldn't tell if it was the doll's lifelike quality or its expensive price tag that made him more uncomfortable.

"Once this is over, maybe you can take the doll back to the store and get them to refund your money," she suggested.

He glanced at the doll again. "I've got a better idea."

She had no idea where he was going with this. "Oh?"

"Yeah, once this is over, I'll give you the doll for Lora. When she gets bigger, she can pretend it's her baby sister, or whatever it is that little girls pretend when they're playing with baby dolls."

She was both touched and impressed. "That's very generous of you," Serena told him.

Carson shrugged. Praise of any sort always left him feeling uncomfortable, like finding out he'd put on two different boots.

"Beats the hassle of trying to get my money back from a salesclerk," he told her.

He was just making excuses. "You're not fooling me, Detective Carson Gage. You might have everyone else thinking that you're this big, hulking tough guy with a heart of steel, but I know better."

For the time being, the doll and its purpose was forgotten. "Oh, do you, now?"

"Yes, I do. Underneath that scowl of yours is a heart made out of pure marshmallow."

"Marshmallow?" he echoed, amused. "Well, that doesn't sound very manly now, does it?"

"Oh, you're plenty manly," she assured him. "But you're also kindhearted and generous, and that's even more important than being manly."

He found himself getting all caught up in this woman that fate had brought into his life. "That all depends if you're staring down the barrel of a gun—or looking into the deep brown eyes of a woman with the kind of wicked mouth you've spent your whole life dreaming about."

She could feel that excitement generating in her veins, the excitement that he could create just by touching her face.

"Oh? And do I have the kind of wicked mouth you've spent your whole life dreaming about?" she asked him, lacing her arms around the back of his neck.

Carson pulled her to him, fitting her body against his. "What do you think?"

His grin was so sexy, she could hardly stand it. "I think you should stop talking and show me."

"I thought you'd never ask," he said, and the next moment, he did.

Chapter 20

Lying there in the dark beside Serena, Carson was beginning to think that the kidnapper had lost his nerve and wasn't going to make a second attempt to abduct the baby.

Two nights had gone by since the first attempt. It was the third night and still nothing.

Carson had to admit that it was getting harder and harder for him to stay awake, allowing himself to take only ten-minute catnaps every few hours as he waited for the kidnapper to make a reappearance.

Maybe it had been strictly a one-shot deal, he thought. Maybe—

Despite the darkness in the bedroom, he saw Justice suddenly sit up. The canine's entire body looked to be rigid and alert. In addition, Justice's ears were moving so that they were directed toward something he heard coming from Lora's nursery.

Tense now, Carson did his best to noiselessly slip out of bed, but Serena still woke up.

Her eyes were wide as she looked in his direction. "Did you hear something?" she asked in what amounted to a stage whisper.

Carson nodded. "Stay here," he mouthed. There was no mistaking that it was an order.

But Serena slipped out on her side anyway. "You might need help," she told him, her voice so low it was all but inaudible.

"Damn," Carson muttered under his breath, but with no less feeling than if the word had been shouted. He didn't have time to argue with her. This could all go south in the blink of an eye and his window to capture the kidnapper was small.

Aware that there was no way he could get Serena to remain in her room, he waved for her to stay behind him, then made his way into the nursery, his weapon drawn and ready in his hand.

Moving just ahead of his partner, Justice saw the intruder first.

The thin, shadowy figure dressed in black had found a way into the nursery. Carson had wanted to make the nursery accessible but not so accessible that the kidnapper smelled a trap.

The intruder was just leaning over the crib and

about to scoop up what he believed to be the baby. At that moment Justice flew across the nursery, grabbing the kidnapper's arm.

Startled, there was a guttural screech from the man, whether out of pain or surprise was unclear.

Somehow managing to pull free from the canine, the kidnapper tried to barrel out of the room. Moving deftly, Carson was quick to block the man's exit. In doing so, he managed to pull off the intruder's ski mask, exposing his face.

"Mark!"

The cry of recognition came from behind him.

Surprised, Carson looked over his shoulder at Serena. It was just enough to throw his timing off, causing Carson to lose the upper hand. The kidnapper immediately took advantage of the opportunity, grabbing Serena's arm and pulling her against him like a human shield. Out of nowhere, a handgun materialized. The unmasked kidnapper held the muzzle against her temple.

Afraid that the canine would jostle the kidnapper and possibly cause the gun to go off, Carson caught hold of Justice's collar, pulling him back to keep the canine still.

"If you don't want her pretty brains splattered all over the room, you'll put your gun down, cop," the man holding Serena hostage snarled.

"Take it easy," Carson told the intruder, speaking in a tranquil, sedate tone and doing his best to harness both his anger and his fear. He shifted his eyes toward Serena. Wanting to keep her calm, he told her, "It's going to be all right."

"Only if you put your gun down and keep holding on to that dog of yours," the man Serena had called Mark snapped. "Now!"

Still holding on to Justice's collar with one hand, Carson raised the weapon in his other hand, pointing the muzzle toward the ceiling.

"I'm putting it down. Don't do anything you'll wind up regretting," he warned the intruder.

"Same goes for you," the man growled. He cocked the trigger.

"I'm putting it down," Carson repeated more urgently, making an elaborate show of laying the handgun down on the floor beside his foot.

The second that Carson's gun was on the floor, the intruder shoved Serena into him. With a startled cry, she stumbled against Carson and Justice.

Carson caught her before she could land on the floor. "You okay?"

She nodded. "I'm fine. Go, get him," she cried urgently.

Carson ran after the man, but as fast as he was, the foiled kidnapper turned out to be faster. The man fairly flew down the stairs and out the back way. Carson kept going until he reached the nearby creek that ran through the property.

That was where Justice lost the would-be kidnapper's scent.

Carson kept searching the area for another twenty minutes, hoping that Justice would pick up the scent again. But after twenty minutes, he was finally forced to give up.

"It's okay, Justice," he said, calling the dog off. "You did your best. We'll get him next time. Let's go back, boy."

When he returned to mansion and went up to Serena's suite, Carson found that she had got dressed. It was still the middle of the night, but it was obvious that she'd given up all hope of going back to sleep.

The second he entered the room, she ran up to Carson. "Did he get away?" she asked.

Despite the fact that she'd asked that, Serena was nursing the outside hope that he'd caught the man and that he was sitting handcuffed in Carson's car, waiting to be transported to jail.

But one look at Carson's face told her that wasn't the case. Mark had indeed got away from him. The nightmare was to continue.

"Yeah," Carson answered darkly. "He ran through the creek and Justice lost his scent."

"You'll get him, Carson," she said with such conviction, it was obvious that she firmly believed that there was no other way for this scenario to play out.

Carson sat down on her bed. Serena dropped down beside him, her courage flagging.

"Who is he, Serena?" Carson asked. "You called him by his name."

"I called him by *a* name," she corrected. She wasn't sure just what to expect or how Carson would handle being told about her connection to the man. "The one he told me when we met."

Carson shook his head. "Still doesn't answer my question. Who is he—to you?" he specified.

"Someone I thought I'd never see again," she told him.

Serena paused, pressing her lips together. It took her a moment to gather her courage together. What she and Carson had was all still very brand-new and fragile. She didn't want to jeopardize it by throwing this other man into the mix.

But she had no choice.

She took a deep breath and told him, "He's Lora's father."

"Oh."

It was one thing to know that Serena had lost her head one night and got involved in what amounted to a one-night stand. It was another to actually meet the other person who had been involved in that evening.

It took Carson a moment to come to grips with the situation, to deal with what he was feeling—a strong flare-up of jealousy. With effort, he tamped it down and forced himself to put it all into proper perspective.

He blew out a long breath. "Well, it's obvious that he's not looking for a happy reunion between himself and his daughter."

Serena felt relieved and threatened at the same time. Relieved because Carson was taking her side in this. She knew that there were men who would have taken the situation and turned it into an opportunity to revile her for foolishly getting intimately involved with a stranger. The fact that Carson didn't, that he didn't lash out at her or upbraid her, making this all her fault, made her feel incredibly relieved and grateful.

"I know it's no excuse," Serena began, "but I'd had too much to drink and—"

"Stop," Carson said sternly. When she did, looking at him quizzically, wondering if she was wrong about him after all, Carson told her, "You don't owe me an explanation, Serena. Whatever happened between you and that man is in the past. What matters is now. We have to move forward from here—and we've got to get that bastard. Do you have any idea where he lives? Is he local or from out of state?"

"Not a clue," she admitted, embarrassed at her helplessness in this matter.

There were other ways to find things out, Carson thought. "I'll get in contact with the county's forensics team, and they can at least dust your suite for any fingerprints that don't belong. Maybe we'll get lucky and Lora's father is in the system."

Serena nodded. Although she was doing her best to get herself under control, she could feel the tears forming. That just made things worse. She didn't want to cry in front of Carson. Crying was something a helpless female would do, and she refused to see herself as helpless.

But despite her resolve, she couldn't find a way to just blink back her tears.

She could feel her eyes welling up so she turned her head away from him. She cleared her throat and said, "Um, maybe I should go down and make breakfast for us."

Rather than let her leave the room, Carson circled around until he was in front of her, blocking her way out. Taking her face in his hand, he tilted it toward him. Looking at her, his suspicions were confirmed. He wasn't about to ask her if she was crying until he knew for certain.

However now that he saw for himself that she was, he wasn't about to fall into that old cliché and tell her not to cry. He just silently took her into his arms and held her.

"We'll get this SOB and find out what his game is. I promise," he told her.

She pressed her lips together, burying her face against Carson's shoulder.

"I'm not going to cry," she told him, her voice breaking.

"Nobody asked you to," he answered matter-of-factly, trying to lighten the moment for her.

"I just want my life back," she told him.

"I know, and you'll get it back," he said, stroking her hair, wishing there was some way he could really reassure her.

Her sigh created a warmth that penetrated right through his shoulder, causing his stomach to tighten. He was prepared to go on holding her for as long as she needed him to.

But the shrill sound of the landline ringing shattered the moment.

He felt Serena instantly stiffen against him, as if the phone call couldn't be anything positive despite the fact that there could be a whole host of reasons why someone might be calling.

He looked over toward the phone on the white antique desk. "You want me to get that?" he offered.

"No, it's my house," she told him, grateful for his offer but refusing to hide behind it. She wasn't going to allow what was happening to diminish her in any way. She'd always been strong and she intended to remain that way. "I should be the one answering my own phone."

Moving away from the shelter of Carson's arms, she crossed over to the antique desk and picked the telephone receiver. "Double C Ranch."

"I know the name of the freaking ranch," the voice on the other end snarled.

It was him, the kidnapper. She would have recognized the man's voice anywhere. Serena instantly made eye contact with Carson, urging him over.

He was at her side immediately, gesturing for her to tilt the receiver so that he could hear what the caller was saying.

Holding the receiver with both hands, she asked, "What do you want?"

Instead of answering her question, Mark said, "I'm calling to find out what you want."

Still looking at Carson, she shook her head, mystified. "I don't understand."

"All right, I'll spell it out for you," Mark said, irritated. "I'm guessing that you want me to disappear and never bother you and that cute little girl, our daughter, again."

Serena cringed. She wanted to shout at the man and tell him that he had no claim to Lora. That Lora *wasn't* his little girl and never would be, that it took more than a genetic donation to make a father.

But she knew she had to remain calm. If she didn't, then Mark would get the upper hand. So she took a deep breath, and as Carson silently urged her on, she told Mark, "Yes, I do." Taking a shaky breath as she desperately tried to steady her nerves, she asked, "How do I make that happen?"

"Easy." His voice sounded almost slimy, she

thought. "All you have to do is bring me a million dollars."

She hadn't been expecting for him to demand that much. "A million dollars?" she repeated, stunned.

As if sensing her reaction, Mark went on the defensive immediately. "Hey, that's not too much for your peace of mind—and your brat. Not to someone like you. Hell, that's practically like petty cash for your family. A million dollars and I'll go away."

She clutched at that phrase. "For good?" she asked.

"Yeah, sure. For good," he told her. "That sound good?"

"Yes." It also sounded like a lie, she thought. "I don't have that kind of cash readily accessible. I need time to gather it together."

"How much time?" he asked angrily.

Her mind scrambled as she tried to come up with a reasonable answer. "At least a couple of days."

"Too much time," he snapped. "You've got nine hours."

"I can't get that much money in nine hours," she cried, thinking of the logistics that were involved.

"*Find* a way," he retorted. "Unless you want to deal with the consequences."

Her eyes met Carson's. He nodded, mouthing instructions and encouraging her to tell Mark that she'd meet him with the money.

Serena let out a shaky breath. "All right. Where and when?"

"Atta girl, now you're playing the game. I want you to meet me in front of that fancy restaurant in town. The one that just opened up. The Barbecue Barn. Be there at three o'clock. Just you and our daughter," he instructed with a mocking laugh. "Bring the million in unmarked bills in a backpack, the kind that schoolkids use. And make sure you come alone. I see anyone else there, if I see anything out of the ordinary, I promise I'll make you very, very sorry—and our kid'll be playing a harp. Understand, princess?"

He was making her skin crawl, as well as making fear skewer her heart. "I understand. If I get you that money, I don't ever want to see you near my daughter or me again," she said with feeling.

"Why, Serena, after everything we've meant to one another? I'm hurt," Mark said sarcastically. And then his voice became deadly serious. "You bring that money, then yeah, you'll never see me again and you and that cop you got guarding your body can go on playing house to your hearts' content.

"Remember, tomorrow, three o'clock. Unmarked bills in a backpack. You can put the backpack in the kid's stroller so nobody'll get suspicious," he added. "You got that?"

"I've got it." Sensing he was about to hang up, she said, "Wait a minute. How do I know you'll keep your word and disappear after you get your money?"

She heard him laugh on the other end. The sound caused another cold chill to slither up and down her spine.

"Well, honey, you're just going to have to trust me on that," he told her.

"Trust you," Serena repeated. What she wanted to do was rip his heart out and feed it to him, but she forced herself to sound docile.

"Yeah, trust me," he said.

Carson was silently telling her to stay calm. But Lord, she was finding it hard to stay civil. "Okay. I'll hold you to that."

He laughed again, the sound slicing through her this time. "You do that, honey. You just do that."

Chapter 21

Serena didn't remember hanging up the phone. She didn't remember crossing to her bed. She *was* aware of her legs giving out from beneath her so that she wound up collapsing onto it.

The next moment, she felt Carson's arm encircling her shoulders. "By this time tomorrow, it'll all be over," he promised.

His words echoed in her head. In the meantime, she thought, she had all this terrible blackmail to deal with. Had to see that disgusting excuse for a human being again for the handoff.

She just wanted this to be over with. "Maybe I should just pay him off," she told Carson.

He looked at her in surprise. "What are you saying? No, don't even think about doing that," Carson told her sternly. He realized that this was her fear talking, but paying this bastard off was not the way to go, she had to know that.

Serena felt as if she was in between the proverbial rock and hard place. "But if paying him off means getting rid of him—" she began.

He stopped her right there. "But that's just it, Serena. You won't. You won't get rid of him. He'll keep coming back, always asking for more money. Blackmailers never stop blackmailing, Serena. They just keep getting greedier." Carson took hold of her shoulders, looking into her eyes and trying to cut through her fear. He had to get her to understand. "You're going to the bank and taking out just enough to fill the top portion of that backpack he wants you to bring. The rest of it will be filled with cut-up newspapers."

"He also said to bring Lora," she reminded Carson.

"You'll be bringing her stand-in instead," he told Serena, nodding toward the crib in the other room where he'd put the decoy doll. "Don't worry," he said, "I'm going to be with you every step of the way."

Much as she wanted him there, she felt she couldn't risk it. "You heard that bastard. He said if he saw anyone with me—"

"He won't," Carson cut in. "Don't worry. I'm very good at my job," he assured her without any bravado. "And after today, he's never going to bother you again." Very gently, he raised her chin so that her eyes met his. "You believe me, don't you?"

"I believe you," Serena answered, although her voice sounded a little hoarse.

"It'd be better with a little more enthusiasm," Carson said, "but I'll accept that."

He kissed her on the forehead in an attempt to comfort her. His lips migrated down to her cheek, then to her other cheek. Before she knew it, the small act of comfort mushroomed into something much more than that.

For the next hour, Serena found solace in his arms as well as sanctuary from some very real fears that existed just beyond the boundaries of her suite.

"That is one hell of a stroller," Carson commented as he helped her load it into her car later that afternoon.

Because they really weren't sure, despite the fact that the blackmailer said he would meet her in front of the restaurant, exactly where Mark might be hidden, Carson didn't want to take a chance on the blackmailer seeing them come into Red Ridge together. So he was driving his own car to town while Serena was going to Red Ridge in hers.

"How much did you say it cost?" he asked her, still looking at the stroller.

Serena flushed, knowing that the pink stroller was

exceedingly ostentatious. It had been a gift from her mother. Joanelle Colton always needed to make a big show out of everything, even something as simple as a stroller. Ordinarily Serena wouldn't have accepted it, except that after what her mother had put her through, she felt the woman did owe her something. The stroller was her mother's way of apologizing. Throwing money at something had always been preferable for her mother than admitting to a mistake.

She'd seen the price tag. There was no doubt in her mind that her mother had left it there on purpose. "A thousand dollars."

Carson let out a low whistle. "For something Lora's going to outgrow in a year? Does your mother always throw money around like that?"

"Always," Serena answered without hesitation, then added as she shook her head, "She thinks it puts people in awe of her."

Carson held his tongue, thinking it best not to say what he thought of that. Instead, he handed the decoy, dressed in Lora's clothes, to Serena.

"Don't forget to put this in the car seat and buckle it up. You don't want this Mark creep to suspect something's wrong," Carson cautioned.

Taking the doll, Serena had to marvel about it again. "This is just *too* lifelike," she told Carson. Not to mention that it felt a little eerie, handling the doll and pretending it was her daughter.

Carson went to the heart of the matter. "Just as long as that doll does the trick and fools Mark, that's all that counts."

She had her doubts about that. "Anyone stopping to look at 'my daughter' will see that it's not Lora—or a real baby."

He had a solution for that. "Then just pull that little cotton blanket down over 'her.' Tell people she's coming down with a cold, and you don't want to take a chance on it getting worse because people are touching her and breathing on her."

Serena got in behind the wheel. "Shouldn't I have left her at home if she's coming down with something?" she asked.

Carson shook his head. "You're overthinking this thing. Just tell them what I said and people will be sympathetic—and they'll leave 'Lora' alone." Standing next to the open driver's-side window, he bent down and put his hand on hers. "Okay, remember to do what we rehearsed. You go to the bank, make that withdrawal, then put the money into the backpack and tuck the backpack into that carry section at the back of the stroller."

Serena was doing her best not to allow her nerves to get the better of her. There was a great deal riding on this. She wasn't worried about getting hurt, she was afraid that Mark would get away again.

She ran her tongue along her very dry lips. "And where will you be again?"

"Out of sight," he told her. "My team and I will be watching you. The second that guy turns up and grabs the money, it'll be all over for him." Carson squeezed her hand. "Trust me."

"I do," she told him. And she did. With her life *and* her daughter's.

Just to reassure her, Carson added, "I won't let him hurt you."

She could see the concern in his eyes. He was worried that *she* was worried. It touched her heart. "I know that."

Even so, Serena was still nervous as she drove from the ranch.

Serena parked away from the bank. She wanted to be able to walk slowly back to her car once she had made her withdrawal from the bank. She reasoned that the longer the walk, the more opportunity Mark would have to steal the backpack from her. What she *didn't* want was to be close enough to her car to have Mark push his way into it, stealing both the backpack *and* her.

The thought galvanized her and made her more determined than ever that the only place Mark was going after today was prison.

"This is rather a large amount of money you're withdrawing, Ms. Colton. Is everything all right?" Edward Abernathy, the bank manager asked.

When she'd initially handed the teller the withdrawal slip, taking the sizable amount from her savings account, the teller had mumbled something about needing to get approval for such a large sum and then went to get the bank manager.

The portly man had greeted her with a profusion of banal small talk ranging from the weather to the state of her family's health. Then he looked at the withdrawal slip as if he hadn't already seen it when the teller had brought it to him.

The bank manager eyed her now, waiting for her answer to his question.

"Everything's fine, Mr. Abernathy," Serena told him with a broad, easy smile. "It's just that I'm dealing with a seller who insists on being paid in cash. I think he's paranoid about having checks bounce on him. It's happened before," she added for good measure.

"That must be some horse you're acquiring," Abernathy marveled. After a beat, he signed his approval for the transaction.

"Oh, it is," Serena assured the man, wishing he would hurry up. It was a quarter to three and she felt that she was cutting it very close. "It's a beautiful palomino. I have to act quickly. There are two other buyers who are interested in the stallion."

"I quite understand," Abernathy said sympathetically. "I'll be back in a moment. Wait right here, please," he told her just before he went into the vault.

He returned a few minutes later.

"Well, there you go," Abernathy said, counting out a number of banded stacks of hundred-dollar bills before tucking all of them neatly into a sack for her. "I see you brought your daughter in with you. Never too young to start them on a sound financial footing. We could open an account for your little darling today if you're interested," the bank manager told her.

"Some other time, Mr. Abernathy," Serena said, then reminded him, "I have that appointment with the seller to keep."

"Of course, of course," the manager answered, watching her tuck the sack into her backpack. He angled his head, as if trying to get a look beneath the screen cover draped across the front of the stroller. "That certainly is one well-behaved baby you have there. I don't believe I heard a single peep out of her this whole time."

"She's a heavy sleeper," Serena replied.

Abernathy chuckled. "Both of mine were screamers. Or so my wife said. I had to work of course, so I missed all that."

"You were lucky," Serena told him, knowing the man was expecting some sort of a comment.

Turning away from the bank manager, she quickly began to make her way to the bank's double doors, anxious to leave the bank before Abernathy could ask any more questions or, worse, ask if he could sneak in one peek at her "baby."

Serena could feel her heart hammering hard as she approached the exit doors.

The bank guard moved toward them at the same time, then obligingly held one of the doors open for her. He tipped the brim of his cap. "Nice seeing you again, Ms. Colton."

"You, too, Eli," she murmured, forcing a smile to her lips.

She had less than five minutes to make it to the rendezvous point.

Focused on getting back to her car in order to make it to the restaurant in time, Serena didn't see him until it was too late. One second, she was walking quickly, pushing the stroller in front of her; the next, she felt a jolt coming from the left and going through her whole body.

It sent her flying to the ground.

Mark had darted out of the alley next to the bank and lunged at her, catching her completely off balance.

Rather than grab the backpack, he grabbed the whole stroller and made a mad dash for the parking lot that was across the street. Obviously intent on upping his game, he was running to his truck with both the money and what he presumed was the baby. The latter was to be his collateral, assuring him of a safe escape.

But he never reached the truck. Instead, he howled in pain as Justice came out of nowhere and caught his arm, dragging him down to the ground.

The second the canine caught him, Mark let go of the stroller. It hurtled toward the street and would have been smashed by an oncoming truck if Finn hadn't managed to grab it just before it went careening off curb.

Several of the K-9 team closed ranks around Mark, although the latter wasn't really necessary. The moment Mark had lunged out of the alley and grabbed the stroller, Carson had transformed from an elderly man dozing on a bench to a K-9 detective and sprinted over toward the blackmailer. Justice had brought the man down, but Carson had been less than half a second behind the German shepherd.

Grabbing Mark by the back of his collar, he shoved him in Finn's direction. "Here's the guy who wanted to steal your niece. I'll be in to do the paperwork as soon as I make sure that your sister is all right and bring her home," Carson told the chief.

"You're making a mistake," Mark cried, appealing to Finn. "The stroller was about to go into the street and I was just trying to catch it before the baby had a terrible accident."

Carson snorted. "You're the one making the mistake if you think any of us are actually buying that lame story," he told the blackmailer.

The next moment, he turned away, not giving the

brazen blackmailer another thought. Right now, all his thoughts were centered on Serena. He swiftly checked her out, his eyes sweeping over every inch of her. She'd got back up to her feet, but Carson wanted to see for himself that she was unharmed.

"Are you all right?" he asked her anxiously.

She didn't bother answering that. Instead, she had an important question of her own. "Is Mark going to be going to jail?"

"Yes. For a long, long time if your brother and I have anything to say about it," Carson answered.

"Then I'm fine," she said, answering his question as she breathed a huge sigh of relief. Turning toward Carson, she looked up at him and very plaintively asked, "Can I please go get my daughter now?"

He grinned. "I'll take you there myself," Carson said.

She remembered what he'd just told her brother. "But what about the paperwork you said you were going to write up?"

"It's not going anywhere," he assured Serena. He glanced over toward the blackmailer. One of the officers was pushing the man's head down and getting him into the back of a squad car. "And neither is Mark." Giving her his full attention, Carson asked, "You ready for that reunion now?" he wanted to know.

"Oh, so ready."

He grinned, expecting nothing less. "Then let's go

see that little girl of yours." Carson let out a piercing whistle. "Justice, come!"

The German shepherd was instantly at his side, ready to follow him wherever he went.

As it turned out, Lora wasn't sequestered all that far away.

Will Taggert, the detective—and father of three—who Finn had entrusted with the baby's safety, had taken her as well as the Colton housekeeper to stay at his family's small ranch.

The second they walked into the room where she and the baby were staying, Alma made no secret of the fact that she was overjoyed to see Serena *and* Carson.

"Did you catch that hateful scoundrel?" the housekeeper asked, excitement and hope clearly written all over her face.

Carson smiled at the woman and nodded his head. "We did. He won't be threatening anyone anymore," he told Alma.

"Oh, thank you!" Alma cried.

Carson murmured something in response, however his attention was focused on Serena. When they had entered the bedroom where Alma and Lora were staying, Serena had instantly rushed over to the cradle and scooped her daughter up in her arms.

"Oh, I have missed you," she told her daughter, pressing the baby against her breast. Serena took in a deep breath. "You smell so good," she said with enthusiasm.

"You're lucky you didn't get here ten minutes earlier, Miss," Alma said with a laugh. "You might not have said that then."

Serena raised her eyes to look at the housekeeper. "Oh, yes I would have. I missed everything about Lora, even changing her diapers." Turning toward Carson, she said, "I don't know how to thank you."

He smiled in response. He had a few ideas on that subject, but nothing he could say right now, not in front of the housekeeper or in front of Taggert, who had just walked into the room. So instead, he said, "Just all part of the job. Right, Justice?" he asked, looking down at the German shepherd.

As if knowing that he was being asked a question, the canine barked in response.

Carson looked over at the housekeeper. "How long will it take you get pack up and get ready to leave?" he asked.

"Is five minutes too long?" she asked.

Carson laughed. "You can have half an hour if you'd like."

"No, Miss Lora and I are all ready," Alma assured him. "No offense," she said to Taggert, "But I never bothered unpacking when we got here."

"None taken," Taggert assured the woman with a laugh.

"Well, if you're all ready," Carson began.

"Then let's go home," Serena said, concluding his sentence.

Carson grinned as he took the suitcase that Alma had produced out of the closet from the woman. His heart swelled as he joined Serena and her daughter.

"Let's go home," he echoed.

Epilogue

Order, to some extent, had been restored.

Serena's daughter as well as the family house-keeper were back at the Double C, as they should be. The rest of Serena's family—her parents and younger sister, Valeria—would be coming back in the morning, Finn had told his sister. Returning on such short notice was "inconvenient" for the older Coltons according to Joanelle. Carson imagined that packing up alone, even though someone else would undoubtedly be given that task, would take some time.

Carson had to admit that he wasn't exactly overly thrilled anticipating Judson and Joanelle's return to the ranch. They had both made no secret of the fact that they looked down on him, as well as down at his family, but in the grand scheme of things, he viewed that as just a minor problem.

Besides, he still had tonight with Serena and tonight, if all went according to his plan, was all he needed.

"You're thinking about your brother, aren't you?" Serena asked, putting her own interpretation to the pensive expression on Carson's face.

It was evening and they were back in her suite at the ranch. For now, Lora was dozing in the other room in her crib.

"No, actually I'm thinking about finding his killer," Carson said. Now that the threat to Serena was over, finding Bo's killer had become his main focus again. "And finding Demi Colton."

She immediately focused on his phrasing. "So now those are finally two separate concerns—aren't they?" she asked hopefully.

Carson smiled. The woman's loyalty was incredible. "If you're asking me if I still think that Demi killed my brother, no, I don't. We're following up on other leads and looking at other suspects." He tucked his arm around her as they lay on her bed. "But that doesn't change the fact that Demi is still out there somewhere, missing—*and* pregnant with my brother's baby. I need to find her," he said seriously, "and bring her in—for her own safety."

Sitting up, Serena shifted so she could look down at him. "Really?" she asked.

"Really," he replied with sincerity. "She shouldn't be alone at a time like this."

Would wonders never cease? "Who *are* you and what have you done with Carson Gage?" she asked playfully.

"I'm right here," he answered, slowly running his hand along the swell of her curves and relishing every sensation that contact created within him. "You're responsible for this, you know, for changing me and making me see things I'd never noticed before."

He watched the warm smile blossom in her eyes before spreading to her lips. That, too, gave him an immense amount of pleasure.

"Then I guess I did a good thing," Serena said.

He laughed, toying with the ends of her hair. "That all depends on whether or not you like the new me."

Crossing her arms on his chest, she leaned her chin against them as she gazed into his eyes. "Oh, I like him. I like the 'new you' a great deal," Serena told him and she pressed a kiss to his lips to show Carson just how much.

"Good, because that makes this a lot easier."

And just like that, Serena could feel herself starting to grow uneasy. Things had been going too well. They'd caught Mark and she'd been reunited with her daughter. That meant that she was due for something to go wrong.

Trying not to sound as nervous as she felt, Serena asked, "Makes what a lot easier?"

Carson took a deep breath. He'd never found himself lacking courage before, but this was an area he'd never ventured into until now. The whole idea of marriage and family was all new to him and there was a part of him that worried it might all be one-sided.

He backtracked. "On second thought, maybe it doesn't."

"Doesn't what?" Serena wanted to know. "What arc you talking about—or *not* talking about?"

Because he was accustomed to always having an escape route for himself, he edged his way into what he was about to say slowly.

"I know that your parents don't much care for anyone who's part of the Gage family—"

"I am not my parents' daughter," she was quick to assure him. "And I don't think the way they do. Now, will you *please* tell me what you're trying to say before *my* daughter wakes up and I have to tend to her—instead of you?" she urged.

As if on cue, Lora began to cry.

"Too late." Serena sighed. She tossed off the covers and began to get out of bed. "I'd better go get her."

Carson caught her by the wrist, holding Serena in place.

"She only gets louder," she told Carson.

He wasn't thinking about the baby right now. "Will you marry me?"

The four words stopped her cold. Did she just imagine that? "What did you say?"

This wasn't the way he wanted to propose. "I didn't want to blurt it out that way, but I was afraid I'd lose my nerve if you—"

She shook her head. She didn't want an explanation. She wanted the words. "Again, please," she requested.

"You want me to ask you again?" he asked, not quite sure this was what she was telling him.

Serena bobbed her head emphatically up and down. "Yes, please."

"I know that your parents don't much care for—"

"Not that part," she told him. "The *good* part."

And then he knew what she was asking him to say. "Will you marry me?"

"Yes!" she cried, throwing her arms around his neck. Then, in case there was *any* lingering doubt, she repeated, "Yes!" And then her eyes suddenly widened. "Listen."

She'd lost him again. He cocked his head, doing as she'd asked. "What am I listening for?"

Her grin all but split her face. "Lora stopped crying. You really do have a magic touch," she told him with unabashed approval.

"Then let me give you a real demonstration of that," he said, bringing his mouth down to hers.

"Yes, please," she said one more time before she lost herself in the wondrous world that only Carson could create for her.

For them.

* * * * *

If you enjoyed this suspenseful novel, don't miss the next COLTONS OF RED RIDGE *book,*

COLTON'S DEADLY ENGAGEMENT
by Addison Fox

*Available in February 2018
from Harlequin Romantic Suspense!*

Get 2 Free Books,

Plus 2 Free Gifts—

just for trying the Reader Service!

HARLEQUIN
ROMANTIC suspense

"Demi Colton is not the sort of woman who murders a guy who can't appreciate her. Especially if that guy was dumb enough to dump her for Hayley."

"So you think it's someone else?"

"Yes, I do. And that someone isn't me," she added in a rush.

That tempting idea snaked through his mind once more, sly in its promise of a solution to his current dilemma.

Catch a killer and keep an eye on Darby Gage. It's not exactly a hardship to spend time with her.

"Maybe you can help me, then."

"Help you how? I thought you were convinced I'm the town murderess."

"I'm neither judge nor jury. It's my job to find evidence to put away a killer, and that's what I'm looking to do."

"Then what do you want with me?" The skepticism that had painted her features was further telegraphed in her words. Finn heard the clear notes of disbelief, but underneath them he heard something else.

Curiosity.

"Fingers pointing at my cousin isn't all that's going around town. What began as whispers has gotten louder with Michael Hayden's murder."

"What are people saying?"

Finn weighed his stupid idea, quickly racing through a mental list of pros and cons. Since the list was pretty evenly matched, it was only his desperation to find a killer that tipped the scales toward the pro.

With that goal in mind—closing this case and catching a killer as quickly as possible   he opted to go for broke.

"Bo Gage was killed the night of his bachelor party. Michael Hayden was killed the night of his rehearsal dinner. One thing the victims had in common—they were grooms-to-be. And in a matter of weeks half the town has called off any and all plans to get married or host an engagement party."

"I still can't see what this has to do with me."

"If you're as innocent as you say you are, surely you'd be willing to help me."

"Help you do what?"

"Pretend to be my fiancée, Darby. Help me catch a killer."

Will Finn find the Groom Killer before the Groom Killer finds him?

Find out in COLTON'S DEADLY ENGAGEMENT by Addison Fox, available February 2018 wherever Harlequin® Romantic Suspense books and ebooks are sold.

www.Harlequin.com